W9-DHI-472

"Richard Stark is the Prince of Noir."

—Martin Cruz-Smith

"One of the most original characters in mystery fiction has returned without a loss of step, savvy, sheer bravado, street smarts, or sense of survival."

—*Mystery News*

"The Parker novels . . . are among the greatest hard-boiled writing of all time."

—*Financial Times* (London)

"No one can turn a phrase like Westlake."

—*Detroit News and Free Press*

"Westlake's ability to construct an action story filled with unforeseen twists and quadruple-crosses is unparalleled."

—*San Francisco Chronicle*

"If you're looking for crime novels with a lot of punch, try the very, very tough novels featuring Parker by Donald E. Westlake (writing as Richard Stark). *The Hunter*, *The Outfit*, *The Mourner*, and *The Man with the Getaway Face* are all beautifully paced [and] tautly composed."

—James Kaufmann, *The Christian Science Monitor*

The Score was also published under the title *Killtown*.

The Score

RICHARD STARK

With a New Foreword by John Banville

The University of Chicago Press

The University of Chicago Press, Chicago 60637
© 1964 by Richard Stark
Foreword © 2009 by John Banville

Originally published by Pocket Books; later reprinted by Coronet Books
under the title *Killtown*. Reprinted in 2001 by Mysterious Press under the
title *The Score*.

University of Chicago Press edition 2009

Printed in the United States of America

15 14 13 12 11 10 09   1 2 3 4 5

ISBN-13: 978-0-226-77104-5 (paper)
ISBN-10: 0-226-77104-0 (paper)

Library of Congress Cataloging-in-Publication Data

Stark, Richard, 1933–
    The score / Richard Stark ; with a new foreword by John Banville.
        p. cm.
    Summary: The fifth Parker novel has the main character planning a score that
involves a dozen professional crooks ready to take over a rich, remote North
Dakota town.
    ISBN-13: 978-0-226-77104-5 (pbk. : alk. paper)
    ISBN-10: 0-226-77104-0 (pbk. : alk. paper)   1. Parker (Fictitious character).
I. Banville, John.   II. Title.
    PS3573.E9S36   2009
    813'.54—dc22

                                                        2008042344

THE PARKER NOVELS
John Banville

It was in the 1960s that Richard Stark began writing his masterly series of Parker novels—at last count there were twenty-four of them—but they are as unrepresentative of the Age of Aquarius as it is possible to be. Try imagining this most hardened of hard-boiled criminals in a tie-dyed shirt and velvet bell-bottoms. Parker does not do drugs, having no interest in expanding his mind or deepening his sensibilities; he cares nothing for politics and is indifferent to foreign wars, although he fought or at least took part in one of them; he would rather make money than love and would be willing to give peace a chance provided he could sneak round the back of the love-in and rob everybody's unattended stuff. When he goes to San Francisco it is not to leave his heart there—has Parker got a heart?—but to retrieve some money the Outfit owes him and kill a lot of people in the process.

The appeal of the conventional crime novel is the sense of completion it offers. Life is a mess—we do not remember being born, and death, as Ludwig Wittgenstein wisely observed, is not an experience in life, so that all we have is a chaotic middle, bristling with loose ends, in which nothing is ever properly over and done with. It could be said, of course, that all fiction of whatever genre offers a beginning, middle, and end—even *Finnegans Wake* has a shape—but crime fiction does it best of all. No matter how unlikely the cast of suspects or how baffling the strew of clues in an Agatha Christie whodunit or a Robert Ludlum thriller, we know with a certainty not afforded by real life that when the murderer is unmasked or the conspiracy foiled, everything will click into place, like a jigsaw puzzle assembling itself before our eyes. The Parker books, however, take it as a given that if something can go wrong, it will, and that since something always can go wrong, it invariably does.

Indeed, this is how very many of the Parker stories begin, with things going or gone disastrously awry. And Parker is at his most inventive when at his most desperate.

We first encountered Parker in *The Hunter*, published in 1962. His creator, Donald Westlake, was already an established writer—he adopted the pen name Richard Stark because, as he said in a recent interview, "When you're first in love, you want to do it all the time," and in the early days he was writing so much and so often that he feared the Westlake market would soon become glutted.

Born in 1933, Westlake is indeed a protean writer and, like Parker, the complete professional. Besides crime novels, he has written short stories, comedies, science fiction, and screenplays—his tough, elegant screenplay for *The Grifters*, adapted from a Jim Thompson novel, was nominated for an Academy Award. Surely the finest movie he wrote, however, is *Point Blank*, a noir masterpiece based on the first Parker novel, *The Hunter*, directed by John Boorman and starring Lee Marvin. Anyone who saw the film will consider Marvin the quintessential Parker, though Westlake has said that when he first created his relentless hero—hero?—he imagined him looking more like Jack Palance.

In that first book, *The Hunter*, Parker was a rough diamond—"I'd done nothing to make him easy for the reader," says Westlake, "no small talk, no quirks, no pets"—and looked like a classic pulp fiction hoodlum:

> He was big and shaggy, with flat square shoulders and arms too long in sleeves too short. . . . His hands, swinging curve-fingered at his sides, looked like they were molded of brown clay by a sculptor who thought big and liked veins. His hair was brown and dry and dead, blowing around his head like a poor toupee about to fly loose. His face was a chipped chunk of concrete, with eyes of flawed onyx. His mouth was a quick stroke, bloodless. (p. 3–4)

Even before the end of this short book, however, we see West-lake/Stark begin to cut and burnish his brand-new creation, giving him facets and sharp angles and flashes of a hard, inner fire. He has been betrayed by his best friend and shot by his wife, and now he is owed money by the Outfit—the Mafia, we assume—and he is not going to stop until he has been repaid:

> Momentum kept him rolling. He wasn't sure himself any more how much was a tough front to impress the organization and how much was

himself. He knew he was hard, he knew that he worried less about emotion than other people. But he'd never enjoyed the idea of a killing. . . . It was momentum, that was all. Eighteen years in one business, doing one or two clean fast simple operations a year, living relaxed and easy in the resort hotels the rest of the time with a woman he liked, and then all of a sudden it all got twisted around. The woman was gone, the pattern was gone, the relaxation was gone, the clean swiftness was gone. (p. 171)

The fact is, though Parker himself would be contemptuous of the notion, he is the perfection of that existential man whose earliest models we met in Nietzsche and Kierkegaard and Dostoevsky. If Parker has ever read Goethe—and perhaps he has?—he will have recognized his own natural motto in Faust's heaven-defying declaration: *"Im Anfang war die Tat"* [In the beginning was the deed]. Donald Westlake puts it in more homely terms when he says that, "I've always believed the books are really about a workman at work, doing the work to the best of his ability," and when in the context of Parker he refers to "Hemingway's judgment on people, that the competent guy does it on his own and the incompetents lean on each other."

In Parker's world there is no law, unless it is the law of the quick and the merciless against the dim and the slow. The police never appear, or if they do they are always too late to stop Parker doing what he is intent on doing. Only twice has he been caught and—briefly—jailed, once after the betrayal by his wife and Mal Resnick, which sets *The Hunter* in vengeful motion, and another time in the recent *Breakout*. Parker treats the law-abiding world, that tame world where most of us live, with tight-lipped impatience or, when one or other of us is unfortunate enough to stumble into his path and hinder him, with lethal efficiency. Significantly, it is the *idea* of a killing that he has never enjoyed; this is not to say that he would enjoy the killing itself, but that he regards the necessity of murder as a waste of essential energies, energies that would be better employed elsewhere.

Violence in the Parker books is always quick and clean and all the more shocking in its swiftness and cleanliness. In one of the books— it would be a spoiler to specify which—Parker forces a young man to dig a hole in the dirt floor of a cellar in search of something buried there, and when the thing has been found, the scene closes with a brief, bald line informing us that Parker shot the young fellow and buried him in the hole he had dug. In another story, Parker and one of his crew tie a hoodlum to a chair and torture some vital information out of him, after which they lock him in a closet, still chairbound, and depart, indifferent to the fact that no one knows where the hoodlum is and so there will be no one to free him.

With the exception of the likes of James M. Cain, Jim Thompson, and Georges Simenon—that is, the Simenon not of the Maigret books but of what he called his *romans durs*, his hard novels—all crime writers are sentimentalists at heart, even, or especially, when they are at their bloodiest. In conventional tales of murder, mayhem, and the fight for right, what the reader is offered is escape, if only into the dream of a world where men are men and women love them for it, where crooks are crooks and easily identified by the scars on their faces and the Glocks in their fists, where policemen are dull but honest and usually dealing with a bad divorce, where a good man is feared by the lawless and respected by the law-abiding: in short, where life is otherwise and better. In the Parker books, however, it is the sense of awful and immediate reality that makes them so startling, so unsettling, and so convincing.

As the series goes on, Parker has become more intricate in motivation and more polished in manner—his woman, Claire, the replacement for his wife Lynn, the one who shot him and subsequently committed suicide, is a fascinating creation, forbearing, loving, nurturing, the perfect companion for a professional—yet in more than forty years his creator has never allowed him to weaken or to mellow. The most recent caper, *Dirty Money*, published in 2008, ends with a vintage exchange between Parker, a woman, and a grifter who was foolish enough to try pulling a fast one on Parker:

> He helped McWhitney to lie back on the bed, then said to Sandra, "If we do this right, you can get me to Claire's place by two in the morning."
>
> "What a good person I am," she said.
>
> "If you leave me here," the guy on the floor said, "he'll kill me tomorrow morning."
>
> Parker looked at him. "So you've still got tonight," he said.

And that is about as much as Parker, or Richard Stark, is ever willing to allow to anyone.

ONE

1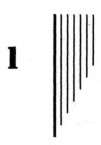

When the bellboy left, Parker went over to the house phone and made his call. He gave the operator downstairs the number he wanted, and waited while the phone clicked and ticked and snicked in his ear. He was feeling impatient, and he was about to go downstairs and put in the call from a pay phone when all the clicking finally quit and a ringing sound started instead.

Parker counted the rings, just as Paulus was doing at the other end, and while he waited and counted he looked around at the room. It was just a hotel room, the same as any. Because it was in Jersey City, it might be a little grimier than most, that's all.

On the eighth ring, the nosy operator came on, saying, "Your party doesn't seem to be answering, sir."

"He moves slow," Parker told her. "Let it ring."

"Yes, sir."

He tensed and relaxed his shoulder muscles, hunching and relaxing, hunching and relaxing. He'd flown up, and being in a plane always made his shoulders stiff. Thirteen, fourteen, fifteen. Sixteen. Where the hell was he?

The ringing stopped, just before seventeen, and a voice said, "Hello?" The voice sounded wary. Paulus had always been a damn fool.

"Hello," said Parker. "I'm here."

"Oh. You made good time."

There was nothing to say to that. Parker waited.

Paulus cleared his throat, and said, "Come on over."

"Now?"

"Sure. We're all here. You got the address?"

If he said no, Paulus would sure as hell give it to him over the phone. Wary one second, big-mouthed the next. He said, "I've got it."

"Fine."

"I'll want to change first. I just got in."

"Anytime."

Parker hung up, shook his head, and lit a cigarette. Paulus would die in jail; it had to happen. He was a good organizer, a good tactician, but he moved through the world like a movie spy, screaming for some cop to look at him twice.

Parker unpacked his suitcase, stripped, took a shower, put on fresh clothes, and left the hotel. Downstairs, he bought a city map at the tobacco counter and sat in one of the leatherette chairs to find his route. Cabdrivers keep a log, so he didn't want to take a cab.

He found Fourth Street, found the block the address should be on, and traced it out from where he was. It was maybe twelve blocks at the most, so he could walk it. If it had been farther away, he would have walked a couple of blocks and then taken a cab to within a few blocks of the address. This way was even better.

He tucked the map in his inside jacket pocket, left the lobby, and started walking. He walked four blocks. Halfway down the fifth block he realized he'd made a wrong turn. He turned around and started back. A guy who'd just come around the corner looked startled, hesitated, made his face blank, and came on. They passed each other, the guy looking straight ahead. Parker had seen that face before, in the hotel lobby.

Fine. Well, it was nice to know before getting into the operation too deep. Paulus had been overdue for years, and this was the time.

Except the guy hadn't looked like law. He was undersized. Most police departments have a height requirement, to boost their self-confidence. And he'd been dressed like a bum, in work pants and brown leather jacket, and wore on his face the gray, pinched look of the loser. He didn't look like law at all.

Parker hesitated at the corner, not looking back. The simplest thing would be to go to the hotel, pack, check out, go to Newark Airport, call Paulus from a pay phone there to warn him, and take the next plane to Miami. If the guy had looked even a little bit like law, that's what Parker would have done. But this way, it was a problem. Before he could know what to do, he'd have to find out what the guy was.

He turned right and started walking again. He'd heard the sound of a train whistle a while ago, one of those diesel blasts, from over in this direction.

The neighborhood went from rundown to nonexistent. Warehouses of brick, boarded-up storefronts, empty lots with paths angled across them. A diner, closed for the night though it was only a little after ten.

Turning corners, Parker had a chance to glance back without being obvious about it. The guy was keeping not quite a block away, walking with his hands in his pockets, trying to look like somebody strolling along with no place in particular to go.

Ahead, a car was coming this way, slowly, the first one in five minutes. It slowed when it reached Parker, and Parker frowned at it, trying to figure. None of this made any sense. He took a quick look back. The guy was still maintaining his block distance, so he and the car had no connection.

Then Parker saw the occupants of the car and relaxed. A guy in his twenties driving, girl of the same age beside him, two little girls standing up on the backseat, looking out the rear window. The car stopped, and the driver stuck his head out the window to say, "Excuse me. Can you tell me how to get to the Holland Tunnel?"

Parker shook his head. "Sorry. I'm a stranger here myself."

"Well, can you tell me how to get the hell out of *here*?" He waved his arms to include the whole neighborhood and looked a little desperate.

Parker thought of the city map in his pocket, but he'd need that later, and he didn't want to waste a lot of time with these people. He pointed the way he'd come, saying, "I think if you go that way you'll come to someplace where there's people."

"Thanks. Thanks a lot."

"Sure."

The car pulled away, and Parker started walking again, first checking the guy, who had slowed down but was still less than half a block back by now. Parker walked at the same speed as before, and the guy gradually fell back to his normal distance.

There wouldn't be a better neighborhood. One car in five minutes, and that guy here only because he was lost. A diner that's closed by ten o'clock at night. No residences of any kind, no twenty-four-hour plants.

In the next block, there were two long warehouses with a loading space between them in near-darkness. Parker passed it without looking in, went down to the corner, turned right, waited a second, and came right back around again.

This time the guy covered it better. He slowed a bit, but that was all.

Parker walked faster than before, timing it. It would work out fine. They'd pass each other right opposite the loading area.

As they passed, Parker on the outside, Parker turned on his left foot and drove a right hand across the side of the guy's jaw. It turned him, threw him off balance, and sent him flailing forward into the loading area to wind up in the shadows there on his hands and knees.

Parker went in after him, to ask him questions and be sure he was getting the right answers. It shouldn't take more than a couple of minutes.

But it wouldn't work that way. There was a clicking sound, and the guy came up with a knife. He didn't waste any time, just lunged.

Parker had no weapons on him but his hands. They were big hands, to go with the rest of him. He moved to the left to limit the guy's knife-arc, pretended a left-hand grab for the knife, and stepped in fast, bringing the edge of his hand in under the guy's jaw.

There wouldn't be any more air going through that throat. The knife fell, and then the guy fell.

Parker had moved as a result of training. Counterattack should be at least as strong as attack. If someone wants to hit you, you hit him. If someone wants to rough you up, you rough him up. If someone wants to kill you, you kill him.

But now, belatedly, he wished he'd pulled that swipe a little. He couldn't get any answers now. The clown shouldn't have reached for a knife.

Parker went through his pockets. Cigarettes, matches, comb, small package of Kleenex, inhaler, unopened box of contraceptives, key chain with three keys on it including one to a General Motors car, nail clipper, wallet. The wallet contained seven dollars in bills, two photos of girls, an unemployment insurance check, and a driver's license. The check and license were both made out to Edward Owen, and the driver's license gave Owen an address in Jersey City.

He hadn't been law, but Parker already knew that. What he'd been, he still didn't know. He put the wallet in his own pocket; maybe Paulus would know. Then he left and walked down to the next intersection and looked at the street signs. There was a streetlight there; under it Parker opened his city map and found out where he was and how to get where he was going.

It was six blocks before he saw anybody at all.

2

Paulus opened the door, looking wary, and then smiled a greeting when he saw it was Parker. "Come on in," he said, holding the door wide. "We been waiting for you." He was short, slender, balding, forty. He was wearing a thin brown suit and a thin brown tie, and he looked like a timid accountant.

Parker stepped into the apartment, took the door away from Paulus and shut it. "The deal's off," he said.

They were standing in a little empty foyer with a spaceship light fixture up above and an Oriental rug below. Paulus blinked rapidly and said, "What? What? What do you mean?"

"Somebody was following me."

Paulus switched to relief again, the way he'd done when he'd seen it was Parker at the door. "Oh," he said, throwing it away. "That doesn't mean anything."

"It doesn't mean anything?"

"I know all about it, Parker." Paulus patted at his arm, trying to get him moving. "Come on in, we're all here, Edgars will explain it to you."

Parker didn't move. "*You* explain, Paulus," he said.

Paulus looked troubled, unhappy. "I think it would be better if Edgars told you the situ—"

"I think it would be better if *you* did," Parker told him. "He's dead."

Paulus now was just blank. "What? Who?"

"Edward Owen. The guy who was tailing me."

"You *killed* him? For Christ's sake, why?" Paulus' tone was intense, but his volume had dropped, as though he didn't want any chance of somebody else in the apartment hearing him.

Parker answered him at normal volume. "He was tailing me. I stopped him to find out why, and he pulled a knife."

Paulus shook his head. "I don't know, Parker," he said. "That's a hell of a thing. I don't know what to tell you."

"Tell me how come you knew I was going to be tailed. Tell me why I was being tailed. And tell me whose idea it was to tail me."

"It was Edgars'," Paulus said, still very soft-voiced. "Owen was his man."

Parker glanced at the entranceway that led deeper into the apartment. "Who the hell is Edgars anyway? I don't remember the name."

"You don't know him, he's never worked an operation like this before."

"Then what's he doing here?"

"He set this one up."

"Oh Christ." Parker shook his head. "The deal's no good," he said. "I can see that already. See you around, Paulus." He reached for the doorknob.

"Wait a second, wait a second." Paulus was getting agitated, but his voice wasn't rising. "Let me explain, will you?"

"You don't have to. This moron Edgars is an amateur, but he's the one setting this job up. He doesn't know me, so he doesn't trust me, so he puts a tail on me to see if I come straight here or do I go see somebody else first because maybe I'm planning a cross."

"You can't blame him, Parker, he—"

"I don't blame him. I don't work with him, either."

A heavy type in a brown suit with a beer can in his hand came through the entranceway, scowling. "What's the holdup here?" He looked at Paulus, and then at Parker. He had heavy black brows, and they were down in a V now to show he was irritated.

Paulus was now really fidgeting. "Edgars," he said, "this is Parker. There's been a—something's come up—there was a misunderstanding."

"What kind of a misunderstanding?" He was trying to act dangerous, but instead he was acting like a ward politician.

Parker waited to see how Paulus would handle it, but Paulus couldn't handle it at all. All he could do was fidget and look around and clear his throat. So Parker said, "You put a man to tail me."

Edgars shrugged. "So what? I want to know who I do business with, that's all."

"He pulled a knife when I called him."

Edgars scowled. "He did? That was stupid; I don't condone that. I'll have a talk with him."

"Not right away you won't."

"What's that supposed to mean?"

"Tell him, Paulus."

Edgars turned his head and scowled at Paulus, waiting. Paulus fidgeted and cleared his throat, and finally he said, "He's dead, that's what he means."

"Dead! You killed him?"

Parker shrugged, and it was Paulus who answered: "He didn't have any choice, Edgars. Your man pulled a knife on him. He didn't know the situation."

"I don't like that," said Edgars. "I don't like that at all."

Parker took the dead man's wallet out and held it out to Edgars. "I took this off him."

Edgars took the wallet and frowned at it. "I don't understand this," he said.

Parker nodded. "I know. See you, Paulus." He reached for the doorknob again.

Edgars said, "Hold on there. Where the hell are you going?"

"I'm out," Parker told him. He pulled the door open.

"Wait." Edgars waved his hands a little. "Will you wait a goddam minute?"

"For what?"

Edgars grimaced, looked again at the wallet he was holding and then at Paulus. Paulus just looked uncomfortable. Edgars said, "Paulus, tell the others we'll be in in a minute."

"Sure thing." Paulus went, happy to be off the hook.

Parker was still standing in the doorway, half in and half out. Edgars said to him, "Wait one minute while we talk, all right?"

Parker shrugged. He'd come this far, he could stick around a little longer. He came back in and shut the door.

Edgars looked around the empty foyer and said, "I wish there was some place we could sit down."

"It doesn't matter."

"All right, I guess not." Edgars looked at the wallet again with distaste and stuck it into a side pocket of his suit coat. Then he gnawed his lower lip and glanced at the entranceway leading into the apartment. Looking off that way, he said, "Maybe Paulus told you, this is the first time I've been involved in something like this."

"He told me. He didn't have to, but he did."

Edgars managed a sour grin and looked out at Parker from under his eyebrows. "Sticks out all over, huh?"

"Yes."

"You and Paulus and the others," Edgars said, "you all know each other, know what to expect from each other. I

don't know any of you at all. When I'm around you, my back
itches."

Parker nodded. "Sure."

"You boys aren't exactly saints."

"So why get involved?"

"A quarter of a million dollars, for one thing. And personal
reasons."

"Paulus is in with you," Parker told him. "And the others.
You don't need me."

"They tell me you're the best. They tell me you can keep
an operation together better than anybody, and you can get
the best men to work with you."

"So why should I work with you?"

Edgars nodded. "That's a fair question," he said. He
reached inside his coat and took out a cigar in an aluminum
tube. While he opened it, he said, "I've made mistakes already, I can see that. Putting Owen on you. Maybe getting
Paulus. I don't know what else." He motioned with his
head, saying, "There's three men in there knew I was
putting Owen on you, knew I'd put Owen on each of them
when they showed up. They didn't act happy about it, but
they didn't stop me. I need somebody to stop me making
mistakes."

Parker shook his head. "That's not my kind of work."

"Wait a minute, now, don't get me wrong. I don't want to
run this deal, for Christ's sake."

"You give a good imitation."

"I've been setting it up, that's all. I've been trying to get a group of professionals together to work *with* me on this, without getting a fast shuffle for me out of it."

"Sure," said Parker. "You had a problem, I see that."

"So what else could I do?"

"Stay all the way out, or come all the way in. Half and half doesn't do it."

"How can I come all the way in until I know what I'm getting myself into?"

"Then stay out."

Edgars shook his head stubbornly. "There's too much at stake."

"Not my problem."

Edgars gnawed his lip. He had the cigar unwrapped now but hadn't lit it. He rolled it back and forth between his fingers. After a minute, he shrugged heavy shoulders and said, "All right. All the way in. I'll give you the setup and then I'll do whatever you say."

Parker considered. "Paulus is in there," he said, "and Wycza. Who's the third?"

"Grofield."

"All right. They're all all right. This is a five-man operation?"

"Oh no. These are just the department heads."

Parker stared at him. "The what?"

"It'll take probably twenty-five or thirty men," Edgars told him.

Parker looked at him as though he were crazy. "You don't have anything at all," he told him. "Twenty-five or thirty men? If a job takes more than four or five men, it's no job. You can put that down as a rule."

"This is a special case."

"Sure it is. Good-bye, Edgars."

"Will you God damn it stop leaving?"

Parker didn't like to do a lot of superfluous talking, but he took the time now to tick off the points for Edgars: "You got an operation needs an army, and the more men in a job the more chance it'll go sour. You got an operation set up by an amateur, for personal reasons. Amateurs get their ideas from the movies, which means flashy and impractical, and personal reasons are no good in a job because they get in the way of clear thinking. Forget it, Edgars."

"God damn it, Parker, you're the man I've been waiting for." Edgars was smiling happily now. He said, "I *know* this is a good solid deal, but I want a professional to *tell* me so, and you're it. All you have to do is hear me out. When I'm done, if you don't think it's workable, then I'll give up the whole idea and I'll pay your fare back where you came from. Fair enough?"

Parker studied him. "Aren't you afraid I'll tell you it's no good, and then go do it on my own?"

"No, I'm not."

"Why not? I'm no saint."

"No, but you're a good businessman."

"What gives you that idea? You don't know anything about me at all."

"I've got a hunch, that's all. Will you listen to the deal?"

Parker thought about it. He didn't see any way an operation requiring twenty-five or thirty men could be workable, and he didn't see any way an operation Edgars was connected with could be workable, but he was here already so he might as well listen. He nodded. "All right."

"Fine. Come on in. You want a beer?"

"All right."

"I'll get it." They crossed the living room, a square sparsely furnished room lit by pole lamps, and Edgars pointed at a door just off the hallway. "They're in there. I'll be right in."

They separated at the hallway, Edgars going for the beer, Parker going into the room with the others. It was a long narrow room with another spaceship ceiling light. The walls were tan, with lighter squares where paintings had once hung, and there was a wall-to-wall green carpet on the floor. Paulus and Grofield and Wycza were sitting around a dining-room table. There was a slide projector on the table and a screen set up at the far end of the room.

Paulus gave him a nervous smile. Wycza, a huge bald man who did professional wrestling when times were bad, waved a beer can in greeting. Grofield, an intense, lean, handsome man who sometimes acted in summer stock theaters, said, "Hail, Parker. Long time no see."

"How are you, Grofield?"

Paulus said, "Are you in, Parker?"

"I don't know yet."

Grofield said, "Herr Edgars is a mysterious type. Did he tell *you* what the job is?"

"Not yet."

Edgars came in, then, with a double handful of beer cans, and Grofield said, " 'All fools in a circle.' "

Edgars laughed. "I hope not, Grofield," he said, and passed the beer around. Then he checked his slide projector, turned it on, and said, "Paulus, would you get the light, please?" He was full of confidence again.

Paulus got up and switched off the light. The projector was beaming a harsh white light at the screen, and it reflected back to give the five men pale faces and vague outlines.

There was a clicking, and the blank face of the screen was replaced by a black-and-white map. Edgars' voice said, "There it is. Copper Canyon, North Dakota."

Parker looked at the map, trying to make sense out of it, but it was just geometric confusion. He lit a cigarette, and waited.

Edgars moved around the table to the front of the room. He had a pointer with him now, like a geography teacher. "This wavy line," he said, and the pointer ran along a U-shaped irregular line that edged the town on three sides, "is the cliffs. The city is built inside a box canyon, with vertical cliffs on three sides, too steep and too tall to be passable. The only way in or out of town is here"—the pointer tapped—"at the open side of the canyon. State highway 22A comes in here, and this here is a spur line of the Dakota and Western Railway. The one road and the railway line are the only means of entry to the town."

Parker silently shook his head. Everything Edgars said

made the deal sound worse. You don't go into a box with only one exit, never.

Edgars kept moving the pointer, tapping here and there. "It's a one-industry town," he said. "Copper. The mine entrances are at the rear of the canyon, here, and the refinery is spread along here. Twelve buildings, storm fencing along here, two gates here and here, both with armed guards day and night, though the plant is working only during the day. There are two banks, here and here, in about the middle of town, opposite each other on Raymond Avenue, the continuation of 22A. There are three jewelry stores, here and here and here, all on Raymond Avenue. The police station is here, on Caulkins Street, near the east gate to the plant."

Parker waited for him to get to the point. He kept telling them about things, banks and jewelry stores and factory gates, but he hadn't got around yet to telling them what he thought they were going to hit. The fan in the slide projector made a humming sound, and Edgars kept on pointing at things.

"The telephone company building," he was saying, "is over here on Blake Street, a block from Raymond. There's a local radio station, with studios here on Whittier Street, but it shuts down operation between midnight and six-thirty in the morning, and there's no one on duty there during the night. The Nationwide Finance and Loan Corporation has offices on the second floor of the Merchants' Bank building. Most stores and other commercial operations are centered along this four-block stretch of Raymond Avenue, with the banks and jewelry stores." The pointer was removed, and Edgars' pale face turned to them. "That's it," he said.

Wycza said, "That's what?"

But Parker already had it. "You're crazy," he said.

"Am I?" Edgars was grinning, pleased with himself. "There are three men on duty in the police station at night, two out in the patrol car and the third in the station to take calls. The plant security force at night is also three, one man on each gate and one man in the front office of the main building to take calls. The banks and jewelry stores and so on have no night security of their own at all. The telephone company has three women employees on duty at night, and the door to their building isn't even kept locked. After midnight, the radio station isn't broadcasting. There is one road and one railway line to watch, to keep townspeople in and reinforcements out. Due to the vandalism of juvenile delinquents, there's been a midnight curfew in town for the last four years."

Wycza was beginning to get it. He said, "Hey, wait a minute, wait a minute."

Grofield laughed out loud.

Paulus whispered, "Sweet Jesus."

"We go in at midnight," Edgars told them. "We pop every safe in town, and we're out by six A.M. Two miles south of where this map leaves off there's the main east–west highway, and from there the whole state network of roads is open to us."

Parker said, "State police."

The pointer slapped the map, down near the bottom. "Substation here on 22A, two miles south of the town limits. State and city are differing political faiths, there's friction. State troopers never patrol north of the city line."

Parker said, "All-night diner."

Edgars shook his head. "None. Curfew, remember? There's a Howard Johnson out on the highway; that's where the troopers go."

Parker shook his head. "Five minutes after we leave, they'll be burning up the phone wires behind us. There'll be a roadblock at the highway before we get to it."

"We can arrange things to give ourselves more time. Break radio and telephone equipment, wreck a truck or two across the road, tie and gag policemen and telephone operators and the rest. We'll have to figure out where we hide out afterwards, of course. We wouldn't want to be on the road too long."

Paulus, over on his side of the table, was shaking his head in wonder. "It could be done," he whispered. "It honest to Christ could be done."

But Parker wasn't satisfied. The operation broke too many rules. Set up by an amateur. Requiring too many men. Involving going into a box with only one way out. And it was just too big and fantastic an idea to begin with, it was science fiction.

Edgars said, "It's time to talk about money. Payday at the refinery is Friday. Thursday night there's approximately sixty thousand in the refinery safe. The two banks should have between fifty and seventy-five thousand in cash each. Give them the low figure, that's a hundred thousand from the two banks. Three jewelry stores, cash and gems, among them they ought to be good for another fifty thousand at the very least. The loan company and department store and other stores and commercial operations, maybe fifty thousand more all told. There's a minimum of a quarter million dollars in that town, maybe more. With twenty-five men on equal shares, that's a minimum of ten thousand a man."

"Ten thousand? That's not much, for the risk."

"That's a *minimum*. There may be more."

Paulus said, "Maybe it could be done with less men, Parker."

"You'd know more about that than I would," Edgars told him.

Grofield said, musingly, "If it could be done at all, it would be fascinating."

Wycza said, "I don't like that state police barracks. And I don't like not having any getaway figured out."

"One thing at a time," said Paulus. "Why don't we think about manpower first?"

Edgars' face, even in the semidarkness, showed an excitement that didn't go with his ward politician features. "The way I thought of it," he said, "would be almost like a commando raid. Each of the five of us would captain a group of five men, including himself. Each of our groups would have specific objectives. My group would take out the police station and radio station and plant security men and telephone company building. Parker's group would go for the refinery safe, with the payroll. Paulus' group would take the Merchants' Bank and Nationwide Finance. Grofield's group would take City Trust and Raymond Jewelers, right next door to it. Wycza's group the other two jewelry stores and the other commercial buildings along Raymond Avenue."

Parker shook his head. They were now talking about his business, his speciality. Whether he took the job seriously or not, he couldn't avoid thinking about it, and about the best way to handle it.

He said, "You don't want to do it that way. You waste manpower. You have four men stand around with nothing to do but watch a fifth man work on a bank vault. You don't need all those men."

Edgars watched him. "How, then? How should it be set up?"

Parker got to his feet and walked to the end of the room. He studied the map projected on the screen, and said, "To begin with, you need four men on stationary plant for as long as we're in there. One at the police station, one at the telephone company, one at the factory front office. Those three to handle any phone calls or anything like that. And the fourth man in a parked car down by the town line, so he can warn the rest of us if anybody's coming in. We'd need walkie-talkies for that. They're cheap, in any Army–Navy store."

"That's four," said Edgars.

Parker pointed at the map. "Five men hit the police station. One stays. That leaves four to hit the telephone company. One stays. Three to hit the west gate of the plant, take care of the guard, get into the main building without being seen by the guard at the east gate."

"No trouble," said Edgars. "The gates are six long blocks apart, and the main building is right near the west gate."

Parker glanced at him. "Any business at night? Truck deliveries or anything?"

"Not usually."

"So there's another man on plant. With a guard uniform on, at the east gate. Sign at the west gate, 'Closed, use other entrance.' That leaves two. One of them has to stay in the office of the main building, and the other one tackles the safe."

"Fine!" said Edgars. "That's fine! Just five men!"

"So far. Everything else you want is on Raymond Avenue, right?"

"Right. So's the west gate to the plant, down at the end of Raymond Avenue."

"I see that. All right, you need four more men, two on each side of the street. One opens the safes, the other one transfers the loot to the cars. We need four cars. One at the town line, for the lookout. One at the plant. Two along Raymond Avenue. Four cars, four walkie-talkies, a lot of guns, ten men."

Edgars moved closer, and for a few seconds his bulky shoulder cast a black shadow on the screen. He moved back out of the way and stood gazing at the map. "Ten men," he said. "I wouldn't have believed it."

"You need three box men. Paulus is good at that, so you need two more. You seem to know the town, Edgars, so you ought to be the lookout."

"You're in, Parker?"

Parker looked at the map. "Not yet," he said. "I want to see a getaway route that makes sense. I don't like the idea of driving four cars out of town past that state police barracks at six o'clock payday morning."

Wycza said, "I don't like that state police barracks at all."

Parker went on, "I want to see a hideout we can get to but the law can't. I want to be sure there's no other way to get information out of that town but what we've already covered, and I want to be sure there's nobody else we have to worry about in that town but what we've already covered."

"We can straighten those points out, Parker," Edgars assured him.

"Then let's do it." Parker looked down at the slide projector. "What's the rest of the slides in that box?"

"His trip to Ausable Chasm," said Grofield.

"Shut up, Grofield." Parker said it quietly, not bothering to look at him.

Edgars said, "Pictures of the banks, the plant gates, the police station, and everything else."

"They'll come in handy some other time. What about getaway route? What about hideout? You got a map of the whole state there?"

"No, I don't."

"You've got to get one. You're from out around there, aren't you?"

"I was." His voice was bitter.

The personal reasons again. Parker didn't give a damn about them. He said, "You get a state map, a couple of them. A road map and a topographical map. You look at them till you find a spot we can hole up. If we leave there at six we've got maybe an hour before the alarm's out. You find us a place fifty miles away or less, that we can get to without being noticed and without leaving tracks, and that the law wouldn't come in after us."

Edgars nodded. "All right, I'll do it."

Wycza said, "What about that goddam trooper barracks? Edgars, ain't there any side road, dirt road, anything at all to take us *around* that barracks?"

"Nothing," Edgars told him. "Flat dead countryside, that's all."

Wycza got to his feet and stretched. His knuckles scraped against the ceiling. He said, "I just don't like that barracks there, that's all."

"Neither do I," Parker told him. "Edgars, switch off that projector, we don't need that map right now. Paulus, give us some light."

When they had light, Parker said, "I don't like four cars going *into* town past that state police barracks, and I don't like them coming out again past the barracks."

Grofield said, "What about holing up inside the town? The old double feint. I've seen you use that a dozen times, Parker."

"It's no good here," Parker told him.

Edgars said, "What is it?"

"It works in some jobs, not this one. You do the job, then make like you're going to run for it. You run maybe two blocks, and hole up. They throw out roadblocks all over the state and wait for you to show up. You don't, so they figure you must of holed up in town. They take the roadblocks down and start looking for you in town, and that's when you leave town."

Edgars laughed. "You're in when they're looking for you out, and out when they're looking for you in."

"Right."

Grofield said, "What's wrong with doing it here?"

"Too small a town, number one. Only one road out, number two. They could put up one dinky roadblock and leave it there for thirty years, till we showed our faces."

Grofield shrugged. "So we have to go past the troopers, that's all."

Paulus said, "Going in's no problem. We can slip in over a couple days."

"So half the townspeople can make you in the rogue's gallery. No good, Paulus. We go in the night it happens and go back out the same night."

"These are details we can work out," Edgars told them.

"We work them out soon," Parker said, "or there's no job."

Edgars said, "Tomorrow morning I'll get the maps. We can meet back here again tomorrow night. Nine o'clock?"

Nine o'clock was all right with everybody. Edgars said, "This thing will work, I know it will. The town's wide open for it, and you people have the knowledge to do it."

"We'll see," Parker told him.

They left one at a time. Wycza went first, and Parker second. Parker walked back to the hotel and went up to his room. He lay down on the bed in darkness and stared at the ceiling, thinking about the job.

It was a crazy one. It broke practically every rule there was. But if the remaining loose ends could be tied up, it just might be workable.

A lot depended on the men. Wycza was all right, steady and fast. Grofield acted sometimes like he didn't take anything seriously, but he knew when to cut that out and get down to work. Paulus was a fidgety type, but first-rate on safes and bank vaults.

But what about Edgars? He had some sort of grudge against somebody in that town, and that wasn't good. Also, he was an amateur at this kind of thing. But in some ways he wasn't an amateur at all. The way he'd reacted to the news about Owen, for instance. Sore at first, but after a while catching on, and then not bringing the subject up again. He was a tough man to figure. First he tried to bluff his way, and then he put all his cards on the table, but there was always the impression there were still a few cards left up his sleeve.

It might be a good idea to find out what Edgars' normal

line was. It just might be that his personal reasons were something that would mess up the operation from the start.

There were still too many doubts; Parker wasn't sure yet whether he wanted to be in this one or not. He didn't really need the dough yet, not for living expenses, but his cash reserve was low. The main reason he'd decided to come on up here and look this over was that he'd been getting bored. . . .

3

He'd been swimming when the call came. Boredom had driven him from the room, and then boredom drove him from the beach. He put his beach robe back on over his trunks, stuck cigarettes and matches in the pocket, and walked through the sand and bodies toward the hotel, which was squatting there like a big white birthday cake.

He was a big man, broad and flat, with the look of a brutal athlete. He had long arms, ending in big flat hands gnarled with veins. His face—it was his second, done by a plastic surgeon—looked strong and self-contained. Women asprawl on the sand in two-piece bathing suits raised their heads to look at him as he went by; he was aware of the looks but didn't respond. It didn't interest him right now.

He knew what the problem was, had known for a couple of weeks now. It had been six months since he'd worked. Inactivity always got to him like this after a while.

He walked on through the sand to the hotel and entered the beach elevator. Two women got on right after him. They were in bathing suits, with towels draped across their shoulders. They were young and good-looking, with the impatient eyes of northern secretaries on vacation. They looked at him and he looked at the elevator boy and said, "Eight." Then he faced front.

Riding up, he didn't think about the women at all, but about the last job. He and Handy McKay had got the statuette for Bett Harrow's father, and a few thousand extra for themselves. Now Handy was retired again, running a diner in Presque Isle, Maine. Parker wasn't retired, didn't want to be retired. But he didn't have anything lined up either. After that last job, he'd spent a while in Galveston, and then he'd gone to New Orleans for a few weeks, and now here he was in Miami. He'd had one woman in Galveston, a couple in New Orleans, but none here. He didn't have the interest.

He got off at the eighth floor and walked down the wide hallway to his room. The telephone started ringing as he was unlocking the door. He went in, shut the door, went across the room, and picked up the phone.

It was the switchboard downstairs. "A message, Mr. Willis," she said. His name here was Charles Willis. She said, "A Mr. Sheer tried to reach you from Omaha, Nebraska. He would like you to call him at your convenience."

"All right. Thank you."

"Shall I place the call for you, sir?"

"No, I'll call later."

"Yes, sir."

He hung up and lit a cigarette and sat down on the bed to think. He knew what the call was all about. It was a job. Whenever anybody wanted to get in touch with him, to offer him a piece of a job, they contacted him through Joe Sheer. Joe Sheer was a retired peterman, an old guy who'd blasted his way into more safes than he could remember and was now living slow and easy in Omaha, with a new face and a fat bank account and a lot of friends like Parker among the boys still working. Joe was the only one who always knew how and where to get in touch with Parker; Parker sent him a postcard every time he moved to a new address. So did half a dozen others; Joe was a good safe middleman and post office.

So it was a job. His instinct was to grab it right away, but he wasn't sure. He had a rule. He never took a job unless he needed it. If you let yourself go, work every chance you got, you just left yourself open for heavy time. Every job carried with it the risk of being grabbed by the law, so the fewer the jobs the less the risk.

He got pencil and paper and worked out his finances. He had seven thousand in the hotel safe here, maybe another ten thousand in bank accounts and hotel safes scattered across the country. The seven thousand was plenty to live on for a while, but ten thousand was too low for a reserve fund. He *could* let it slide a few more months, on what he had, but it might be safer in the long run to stoke up the reserve fund now, when he had the chance.

He was making excuses for himself, and he knew it. But he needed to be working, he needed to have something to think about, even more than he needed to build up his reserve cash supply.

He could look into the job, anyway. It might not be any good. Just about half the jobs he was invited on looked good to him. The rest had something wrong with the setup, or the personnel, or one thing and another, and he stuck around only long enough to hear the story. So there was an even money chance that he wouldn't be taking this job anyway, but at least he'd have something to think about for a couple of days.

He got to his feet and changed from robe and trunks to slacks and sports shirt, and then left the room again. He took one of the front elevators this time, rode down to the lobby, and left the hotel. A call like this one wasn't made through a hotel switchboard.

He crossed the boulevard and took a side street away from the beach. The hotels on the inland side of the boulevard were a little smaller and a little grayer than the beachfront hotels; behind them stretched a declining expanse of tourist courts and efficiency apartments and motels. After a while there were supermarkets and liquor stores and bars.

Parker went into a bar and got five dollars in change from the bartender, then went to the phone booth in back to make his call. When he closed the booth door, a little fan went on over his head, but it didn't do much good. He began to sweat right away.

It took a while to get the call through, and then he had to

pump quarters and dimes into the box before he could talk. He said, "Charles Willis here."

"Good to hear you, Chuck." Sheer had an old man's voice, with something cheerful in it. "How's the weather down there?"

"Hot."

"Still on vacation, eh?"

"I'd go back to work if anything came along."

"I was talking to a fella in your line the other day. Paulus, you know him?"

"Sure."

"Him and Wycza and some others, they're opening a branch office in Jersey City. Maybe they could use another field man."

"The main operation going to be in Jersey City?"

"No, I don't know where the head office is. That's just a branch, to get organized."

"I might send them a résumé. What's the address?"

"Three nine nine Crescent, four A."

"Are they open for business yet?"

"You probably ought to call first and check. The number's 837-2598."

Parker was writing it all down. "I wouldn't call long distance," he said. "I'd just send them a résumé. What do they pay, do you know?"

"That I don't, Chuck, sorry. Ought to be good wages, though, the way Paulus was talking."

"Is he the sales manager?"

"No, I don't think so. There's some sort of regional manager setting things up, the way I get it."

"I might look into it. Thanks for thinking of me."

"Anytime, Chuck. Send me a bathing beauty."

Parker left the booth, had a beer to get rid of some change and to cool off a little, and then walked back to the hotel. He phoned down to have his bill made up, made a reservation on a jet flight to Newark, and packed. He left the hotel room, and five hours later he walked into the hotel room in Jersey City. Then he met Edgars and heard the proposition.

Knock over a city. A whole goddam city.

It was so stupid it might even work. But it would have to be planned right. This one would have to be planned right on down to the shoe leather.

If Edgars wouldn't louse it up some way.

If they had every communications outlet in town figured.

If they could work out a sensible getaway route to a reliable hideout.

If they could get the right men.

If they could think of every possibility.

Right now, it was still just an idea, not a job yet. Maybe it never would be a job. He'd sleep on it.

4

"Fire department," said Parker. "They got to be in touch with other fire departments around the state."

Edgars frowned around his cigar. "God damn it," he said. "I forgot about that."

They were sitting around the dining-room table again, the five of them. Paulus was taking notes. The screen was up, at the far end of the room. The projector stood slightly up-angled on the table like a naval gun, but they weren't using it right now, so the spaceship ceiling light was on.

Wycza said, "That's another man. To sit by the phone in the firehouse. And now we got firemen to keep on ice. Firemen, policemen, gate guards, telephone girls, the whole goddam town."

Parker nodded. "There's too many angles."

Paulus looked up from his note-taking. "Why not just take

the payroll? In and out fast. We five here could do it, keep it simple and neat."

Edgars shook his head. "No good at all," he said. "Don't you remember that map?" He put his hands down on the tabletop. "Here's your payroll, with a cliff in back, a cliff on the right, a cliff on the left, and the whole city spread out in front. You couldn't get through the city in the first place, and if you did there's still only one road out."

"Past that goddam state police barracks," said Wycza.

Edgars said, "That's right. Nobody's ever even tried to steal that payroll, because it just can't be done."

Parker said, "It's no good trying for any one thing in that town. The payroll or a bank. You've got to hit the whole town, or nothing."

"What about the fire department?" asked Paulus. "That's an eleventh man."

Grofield said, "Not necessarily. Give them a diversion."

Wycza looked at him. "A what?"

"A fire."

They all looked at him. Grofield grinned and shrugged, then turned to Paulus, sitting next to him on the right. Still grinning, he drove his left fist at Paulus' face. Paulus cried out and threw his hands up. Grofield's left stopped in midair, and his right hand dug painfully into Paulus' ribs. "Feint," he said. "Feint and attack. Give the boys of the fire brigade a real ripsnorter to think about, in a quiet corner of town where they'll see no evil, hear no evil, get wise to no evil."

Paulus said, "You keep your hands to yourself, buddy."

He'd dropped the pencil he was taking notes with, and stooped over to get it.

Grofield grinned at his back. "Just a graphic illustration of the point, dear heart," he said. "Essence of theater."

"That's not a bad idea," said Edgars.

Parker shook his head. "A six-hour fire? They'll be done before we are."

Wycza said, "We need an eleventh man, that's all."

"We need one, anyway," Parker told him. "We need one man loose, to troubleshoot anyplace something unexpected comes up. If we need another one for the fire department, that's twelve." He turned to Edgars. "Where's the firehouse?"

"Across the street from the police station."

Paulus said, "So we've *got* to cover them. Twelve men. We're going right back up to twenty-five again."

Edgars took the cigar out of his mouth and looked insulted. "Why? Twelve men, what's so bad about that? Twelve men to take a whole city."

"Maybe we're not done yet," Paulus told him.

"Night people," said Grofield, "that's what we've got to think about. Who are the night people? Cops, firemen, telephone girls, we've got them. What about milkmen?"

Edgars shook his head. "They're union, they deliver in the daytime."

"Post office," said Grofield. "They've got to have somebody around for special-delivery letters. Western Union office. Railroad station. Cabdrivers."

"You don't have to worry about cabdrivers," Edgars told

him. "I told you there was a curfew. There's no taxi customers after midnight."

"What about emergencies?" Grofield asked him. "Ladies having babies, children swallowing pins, men with appendicitis. Ambulances racing back and forth amid the booming safes."

Parker said, "That's right. Hospital. You got a hospital in this town?"

"No. The fire department has an ambulance, to take any emergency cases to the hospital in Madison, fourteen miles away on the highway."

Paulus said, "So the fire department man covers the ambulance, too."

Parker asked Edgars, "You know the train schedules? Anything going in or out between midnight and six in the morning?"

"No. It's just a spur line in. There's one passenger train a day, and two freight trains. The railroad station is closed between eight at night and eight in the morning."

"Good," said Paulus. "That takes care of the railroad station."

"Western Union," said Grofield. "Post office."

"The post office closes," said Edgars. "I'm sure it does. I don't know what they do about special-delivery letters. Maybe they drive them in from Madison."

"But Western Union?"

"They've got an office on Raymond Avenue. I don't know if it closes nights or not. I should, but I don't."

"We have to know," Parker told him. "You got a contact in that town?"

"No."

"If everything else closes down," said Paulus, "the Western Union office probably does, too. They wouldn't have much business at night."

"No business at all," said Edgars. "Most likely any telegrams that come at night are driven in from the Madison office, the same as special-delivery letters. I can't remember if I've ever seen the Western Union office open at night, but I don't see why it would be."

"We have to know," Parker repeated. "If it's open, it's got to be covered, and that means another man."

"The only way to find out," Edgars told him, "is to go to Copper Canyon and look for yourself."

"I know."

"I'll write it down," said Paulus.

"More night people," said Grofield. "Who can think of more night people? You say there's no all-night diner?"

Edgars shook his head. "No. No business stays open at all, because of the curfew."

"That's a very small-town thing, a curfew," said Grofield. "Big cities talk about it, but small towns do it."

Wycza said, "What about a newspaper?"

"A weekly," Edgars told him. "It comes out on Thursday, for the convenience of the shoppers."

"No reporters on at night?"

"No. Most of the paper is written by the secretaries of women's organizations."

They were all silent, then, all trying to think of other people who might be out and around late at night. After a minute, Paulus said, "That's it, then. We need another man, to cover the fire department. And we have to find out about the Western Union office."

Wycza said, "What about the getaway?"

"I got the two maps like Parker suggested," Edgars answered. "There's no other way to get out of town except the road, but I think I've found the hideout."

"I don't like that barracks," Wycza said.

Grofield said, "An idle thought. What about the mine?"

They looked at him. Edgars said, "What about it?"

"Are there no entrances other than at the back of the canyon? No shafts leading out anywhere else? No emergency exits?"

Edgars shook his head. "I don't think so. All the shafts go straight down in from the canyon. There's no reason for any other way in."

"Just a thought." Grofield smiled. "I visualized us trundling away on ore carts with the loot, like the seven dwarfs."

"We have to go past the barracks," Parker said. "There's no other choice. We space it so we don't have a convoy go by all at once, and we'll be all right." He turned to Edgars. "What about the hideout?"

"Let me get the maps." He stood up. "More beer?"

They all wanted more beer. He went away and came back with a double handful of beer cans. He set them down on the table, and took two maps out of his hip pocket. He spread them out on the table, covering most of the table's surface. One was a state road map, the other a topographical map.

They were all standing now, leaning over the maps. Edgars pointed to the topographical map, saying, "See, there's Copper Canyon. That's a mesa back of it, it gradually levels down again. Out in front, it's lowland for over a hundred miles. Down in here is one of the coal beds, lignite coal. This is just about the edge of the Badlands here. This whole section here is full of lignite coal. Some of it's right out on the surface, burning, been burning for years."

Parker didn't give a damn about lignite coal burning or not. He said, "The hideout."

"I'm getting to it. Like I said, this section here is just about the edge of the Badlands, so it's away from the tourist areas and it's away from the mining operations. There was a strip mine working there a few years ago, but they're gone now; they cleaned out what they could get and left. There's an eighty-foot-deep ravine there now, where they scraped the topsoil off and took the coal out. There's nobody there now at all. There's some kind of sulphur by-product oozes out of the ground, pollutes the water, and stinks the place up, so nobody goes near it. But the mining company built a road into it, and their old sheds should still be there, on the lip of the ravine."

"What kind of road?" Parker asked him.

"Dirt. But passable. They brought trucks in and out."

"How do we get to it?"

Edgars switched over to the other map. "See, here's 22A here, coming out of Copper Canyon. We pick up the highway here, and turn left. Then there's this smaller road here, goes off to the right. We'd be on the highway maybe three miles. This small road we stay on for five or six miles, and then the mining company road goes off that to the left."

"This land is all flat here?"

"It's plains land. Rolling land."

"When we turn off the small road on to the mining company road, can we be seen from the highway?"

"No, not a chance. That's wild country in there, and there's some trees."

"How many miles in on the mining company road?"

"Maybe seven."

"And how many miles from Copper Canyon to the highway?"

"Eight."

Parker ran his finger along the map. "Eight miles to the highway, then three miles to the secondary road, six miles to the mining company road, seven miles in from there. Twenty-four miles."

"Looks good," said Paulus.

Grofield said, "How much traffic on that highway early in the morning?"

"Six in the morning?" Edgars shook his head. "None."

"Good," said Paulus. "We won't be seen."

"No good," Parker told him. "If anybody does see us, we'll

stick out like a sore thumb. Four cars in a row on an empty highway, all turn off together. All it needs is one trooper to see us."

Wycza said, "What about a truck? A big-ass tractor trailer. We stash it outside of town and switch to it when the job's done."

"Too much loot to be transferred."

Grofield said, "We bring the tractor trailer into town with us. Instead of loading two cars along the main drag, we load the tractor trailer. Then we have a car at the plant, the way we figured, and another car parked near the town line for a lookout. We leave that one, and just take the tractor trailer and the other car. They space five minutes apart, and it doesn't look so bad. You see tractor trailers all hours."

Wycza said, "All right, that's even better."

"It would work," said Edgars. "It would sure work all right."

Parker stood looking at the two maps and thinking it over. Twelve men. In at midnight, out by six in the morning. Everything covered, if they'd thought of everything, and if Edgars had his facts straight.

It was a job. It would work. The thing looked like idiocy at first, but it would work.

He nodded. "All right," he said. "Who's financing?"

Edgars looked blank. "Financing?"

"This is going to cost," Parker told him. "Walkie-talkies, the truck, the cars. Transportation out there. Food and water

RICHARD STARK

stashed at the hideout ahead of time. Guns. It'll cost dough
to get this thing set up."

Edgars still looked blank, and now a little worried besides.
Paulus explained it to him. "Every job has to be financed," he
said. "Whoever puts up the dough gets it back doubled if the
job works out."

"You mean, one of us?"

Parker shook his head. "No. It's better to get your financing done by somebody outside the operation. Otherwise the
man who put the money in tries to run things."

"This is all new to me," Edgars told them.

"I'll go over to New York tomorrow," Grofield said. "I've
got a couple contacts over there. How much you figure?"

Parker frowned, thinking it out. "Four thousand," he said.

Edgars said, "Four *thousand*!"

"I told you, it's going to cost. The truck, the cars, the—"

"Why not just steal the truck?"

"You want to leave Copper Canyon in a hot truck on every
state trooper's list for a thousand miles around?"

"You mean, you just go to a used-truck dealer and buy a
truck?"

"No, not that either. Then you got problems with registration. There's outlets where you can pick up a mace pretty
cheap."

Edgars couldn't seem to get the bewildered look off his
face. "A mace? What's a mace?"

"A car with papers that look good and license plates that
look good."

"But they aren't really?"

"They aren't really."

Edgars sat down, shook his head, and drank some beer. "I didn't know there was this much to it," he said. "How many people have to know about this deal?"

"Just the ones in on it. Twelve men."

"But Grofield's going to go talk to somebody about financing, and you're going to buy a stolen truck—"

"The man that finances doesn't know what the job is. Just that there's a job, and it needs so much to get set up, and it should be done by such and such a date."

"How you going to get a man to put money into a deal without knowing what it is?"

"He relies on the men in the deal. If he knows them, knows they do good work, he takes a chance on them."

"What about where you buy the truck? You don't tell him anything either?"

"Why should we?"

Edgars shrugged and spread his hands. "All right," he said. "You people know what you're doing."

"We rather hope so," said Grofield. He turned to Parker. "Come along with me tomorrow, okay? I know one guy in particular, he knows you. If he sees you're in he'll cover us with no trouble."

"All right."

"Now," said Paulus. "About personnel."

They all sat down at the table again, and Edgars cleared away the maps. Parker said, "We need three jug men. You're one, Paulus. You work one side of Raymond Avenue, and Wycza can carry for you. Grofield, you'd be a good man for the phone company, keep the ladies from getting too scared."

Grofield smiled thinly. "You know my boyish charm," he said. "I'll be happy to keep the ladies company."

"Edgars, you ought to be lookout at the town line. You know the town, know the circumstances there. You can figure anything that moves quicker than anybody else."

Edgars said, "I thought I'd be better off taking care of the police station. I know a little something about police procedure there, I could probably fake it better than anybody else if a phone call came in or anything like that."

Parker shrugged. "Wherever you think you'd do the most good."

"Police station."

"All right." Parker turned to Paulus. "You got a list of the jobs? Wait a minute, the other two juggers first. I'll see if I can get Handy McKay. He could get in at the payroll as fast as anybody I know." He looked around the table. "We need another jugger. A vault man. Any ideas?"

Paulus said, "What about Rohatch? He's a drunk, but he's good at vaults."

Grofield shook his head and said, "I heard he died. The liver got him."

Wycza said, "I worked once or twice with a fella named Kemp. Any of you know him?"

"He's unreliable," said Paulus primly. "He's on the needle. He may even be in jail by now for all I know."

Wycza said, "All right, forget him. How about Wiss? Little guy, but fast."

"I've worked with him," said Parker. "While I was having that trouble with the Outfit. He's a good man."

"I'll see can I get in touch with him," said Wycza.

Edgars said, "What about you, Parker? What's your job going to be?"

It was Wycza who answered. "He ought to be the loose one, the troubleshooter."

Edgars nodded. "Fine by me."

"I'm writing all this down," said Paulus.

Parker said to him, "What other jobs?"

"You want Wiss to work the other side of Raymond Avenue, right? So you need someone to work with him, like Wycza's working with me."

"We'll let him pick his own sideman. Lookout's next. We want somebody fast, and cool."

"Salsa," said Grofield. "That bastard could hunker down in Times Square and disappear. You'd never see him, and he wouldn't move for a hundred years if he had to. But when it was time to move, zoom."

"I know Salsa," said Parker. "He's a good man."

"I'll get word to him."

Parker turned to Paulus. "What's left?"

"Just three. Fire department, gate guard, and plant office. Three men in place."

"I know the guy for the gate guard," said Wycza. "Pop

Phillips. He wears some kind of uniform just about every job he takes."

"Good old Phillips," said Grofield. "Pop Phillips, the sweet old rummy."

"He don't drink when he's on a job," Wycza told him.

"You're right, he doesn't. But he's got bad breath."

Parker said, "Shut up, Grofield. Okay, Wycza, get Phillips. Now we need two more."

"The Chambers brothers," said Paulus.

Grofield shook his head. "Ernie's in jail."

"What the hell for?"

"Statutory. You know how those hillbillies like young meat."

"What about his brother?"

Grofield shrugged. "He's as good as the next man."

"I'll get in touch with him," said Paulus, and wrote it down.

Parker said, "If Littlefield's still working, he'd be a good man for the plant office."

"I worked with him last year," said Wycza. "He was still going strong then."

"Get in touch with him, will you?"

"Right."

Paulus looked up from his notes. "That's all," he said. "Except Wiss' sideman. He can get him himself."

"Day after tomorrow," said Parker. "Here again. Nine o'clock."

Edgars got to his feet and rubbed his hands together. "This is going to work out," he said. "It's going to work out."

They left the apartment one at a time. This time Parker waited, to be the last out. When he was alone with Edgars he said, "Something I wanted to ask you."

"What?"

"What about Owen?"

"Owen? What about him?"

"He's dead."

"I know that." Edgars was frowning at him, but then his face lit up with understanding. "Oh. You mean, what's my attitude?"

"That's right."

"I couldn't care less, Parker. He was just a bum I picked up here in town. He was more stupid that I thought, and exceeded his orders. That's over with."

Parker nodded. "All right," he said. "See you day after tomorrow."

"Right."

Two

1

Parker pumped change into the phone box and listened to it booming. Then he waited.

He was in a phone booth next to a gas station. June sunlight poured down everywhere. Grofield was in his car, a three-year-old black Rambler sedan, parked just down the block; they were on their way over to New York to see about financing, and Parker wanted to make the call now, early, to give Handy time to get here.

The booming was replaced by a ringing sound, and then by a male voice. Parker said, "Arnie LaPointe, please." You couldn't get in touch with Handy direct. Like Parker with Joe Sheer, Handy had a middleman.

The voice said, "Speaking."

"This is Parker. If you see Handy McKay around, ask him to give me a call."

"I'm not sure I'll see him."

"This a pay phone, I can't hang around too long."

"I just don't know when I'll see him."

"When you do, tell him I saw the monk and he's still mourning." That was a reference to the last job they'd worked together, so Handy would know it was him.

"If I see him, I'll tell him. What's your number there?"

"This is Jersey City. The number's OL 3-4599."

"I don't promise anything."

"Sure."

Parker hung up and waited. He pushed open the booth door to get some air, and lit a cigarette. He could see Grofield sitting in the car, relaxed and easy. Grofield was too playful sometimes, but he knew when to cut that out. The operation was shaping up to have good men in it, and with good men in a deal it was tough for the deal to go sour. Not impossible, but tough.

A gas station attendant in blue overalls came over, wiping his hands on an orange rag. He said, "Anything wrong?"

"They're calling me back."

"Okay." He went away again.

Parker finished his cigarette, flicked it out into the street. He leaned against the side of the booth, folded his arms, and waited some more.

He waited fifteen minutes and then the phone rang. He picked it up and said, "Charles Willis here."

It was Handy McKay's voice: "What's the story?"

"Thought you might like to come visit. I got a new place."

"Social call?"

"We might work a little."

"Not for me, remember? I retired."

"You might like the weather here. And there's thousands of things to see. Maybe twenty thousand."

"Don't tempt me. This time I'm retired for good. I got the diner going, and I'm settling down, and everything's fine."

"I was looking for company. Open a can or two with me, you know?"

"Yeah?" There was a pause, and he said, "What about Wiss? He's good company."

"He's already coming."

"Oh yeah? What do you want, a crowd?"

"Yes."

"Jesus, now you got my curiosity up. But it's still no soap. Wait a second, how about Kerwin?"

"That's an idea. You just don't want to travel, huh?"

"Not anymore. I'm settled down."

"All right. I'll drop in sometime."

"Do that. I'll fry you an egg."

"Sure."

He hung up and left the phone booth and walked down to Grofield's car. He slid in and said, "McKay's out. He's retired."

"Again?"

"This time he says it's for good. He suggested Kerwin."

"I don't know him."

"He's a good man."

Grofield shrugged. "I'll take your word for it. Call him."

"He lives in Brooklyn. I'll call him from the city, after we see your man. Who is he, by the way?"

"Ormont. Chester Ormont."

"Four thousand might be steep for him."

"We'll see."

Grofield started the engine, and they drove away from there. They went through the Holland Tunnel into the city, and took the West Side Highway up to 72nd Street, and then crosstown through the park to the East Side. Grofield parked illegally on East 67th Street, between Fifth and Madison, and they walked down the block to the address. It was a fashionable brownstone, with a doctor's shingle in the window. They went up the stoop and inside, into the dimness, and there was a nurse in a white uniform at a desk. She smiled impersonally and said, "Name, please?"

"Grofield. About my back."

"You've been to see the doctor before?"

"Yes."

"Have a seat, please, the doctor will be with you in just a minute."

They went into the waiting room, a large airy room done in Danish modern. Two stuffed matrons sat in opposite corners of the room, like welterweights between rounds. One was reading *Fortune*, and the other was reading *Business Week*. Grofield picked up a copy of *Time* from the central table, and he and Parker sat down to wait.

After about five minutes, the nurse appeared and took one of the women away with her. A little while later a white-haired old man came in on a cane and took the absent woman's seat and *Fortune*. Sometime after that the other woman was escorted away by the nurse.

They waited about forty minutes, and then the nurse came to the door and said, "Mister Grofield?"

Grofield said, "Come on." He and Parker followed the nurse out of the waiting room, down a cream-colored hall, and into an office. There was no one in the office. The nurse said, "Doctor Ormont will see you in just a minute." She went away.

They sat in brown leather chairs and waited. They could hear a murmuring from somewhere else on the first floor. Five minutes went by, and then the door opened and a heavy impatient-looking man with pink scrubbed hands came in. He smiled sourly at them, and said, "How are you, Grofield?" and went around behind his desk.

"Just terrible, Doctor," said Grofield. "I've got this terrible pain in my back."

"Never mind that," said the doctor. "This office isn't bugged."

Grofield burst out laughing. "Doctor, you're priceless!"

The doctor didn't get it, and didn't want it. He looked at Parker and said, "You remind me of somebody."

Grofield said, "This is Parker, with a face job. Not just the nose, the whole face. What do you think of that?"

"Parker, eh? Who did the job?"

"A doctor out west," Parker told him. "You wouldn't know him."

"He did a good job." The doctor switched his attention to Grofield. "You've got something on, eh?"

"So we have. We need financing."

"Obviously. This isn't a social call."

"Of course not. It's this pain in my back, it's killing me."

Parker said, "Cut it out, Grofield."

"Right you are." Grofield sobered, and said, "We need four G's."

"Thousand? Four thousand?"

"Right the first time."

"That's a hell of a bite." The doctor frowned, and stared at papers on his desk as though one of them had written on it the answer to a question that had been bothering him for months. "How long?" he asked.

"Couple of weeks. Maybe a month."

"Anyone else I know in on it?"

"I don't think so. Just me and Parker."

"But there's others in."

"Oh sure."

The doctor considered again, then looked at Parker. "You're in it?"

Parker nodded. He knew Ormont wasn't very bright; the only thing to do was wait till he got everything straightened out inside his head.

Ormont said, "When do you need it by?"

Grofield shrugged. "Now. As soon as possible."

"Tomorrow afternoon, the earliest. The absolute earliest."

"All right, fine. I'll come in and get it."

Ormont nodded heavily. "Tomorrow afternoon. Two o'clock. I won't be having office hours then; just ring the bell."

"Will do."

They all got to their feet. Ormont said, "Good to see you again, Parker. The face is a very good job."

Parker nodded again. There wasn't anything to say; he'd never been any good at small talk.

Ormont said, "Sorry to keep you waiting the way I did. But we've got to keep up appearances. My nurse isn't in on it."

"That's all right."

They went out. When they were back in the car, Grofield started laughing again. "This office isn't bugged! Parker, if you had a sense of humor you'd bust a gut right now. This office isn't bugged! I wouldn't take a million dollars for that man."

Parker lit a cigarette and waited for Grofield to get over it.

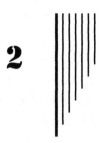

2

Twelve men made the dining room uncomfortably full. Edgars had set up folding chairs for the extras and had distributed beer. Then he and Parker and Paulus had taken turns filling the new men in on the operation. Edgars had run his slides, showing them the map, and also the photos of Raymond Avenue and the banks and the two gates to the plant and the police station and everything else. The room had filled with smoke, even with both windows open.

Handy McKay was the only one selected who hadn't chosen to come in at least to listen. The rest were all there. Wiss and Kerwin, the other two safe and vault experts, both small, narrow men with an intense and concentrated look. Wiss had brought, to work with him, a rangy fortyish man named Elkins, with whom Parker had worked in the past. Chambers was there, a big awkward-looking hillbilly with a brother in jail for statutory rape. And Pop Phillips, an old guy who looked like Hollywood's idea of a night-watchman. And Littlefield, a stocky man in his fifties who looked as though he made his living selling gold-mine stock. And Salsa, in his late thirties, tall and slender, who looked like a gigolo and used to be one.

When the talk and the slide show were finished, and when Edgars had distributed more beer, Paulus asked if there were any questions. Wiss said, "One. What's the split?"

"Even," Paulus told him. "Every man a twelfth."

"That's not the regular way."

Parker said, "This isn't the regular job. It's more men than usual, and more things to do."

Wiss shrugged. "It don't matter to me. What's a twelfth of two hundred fifty grand?"

"That's minimum," said Edgars, "just a minimum."

Paulus said, "A little over twenty thousand."

Wiss said, "Twenty thousand's all right."

Littlefield, looking like a man at a board meeting, said, "You got financing yet?"

"Picked it up yesterday," Grofield told him.

"How much?"

"Four G's."

"That's eight thousand off the top. You couldn't cut it any closer than that?"

Parker said, "You heard the setup. You got any way to shave it?"

Littlefield shook his head. "I guess not. But eight thousand's a big bite."

"Less than seven hundred a man," Paulus told him.

Elkins, the man Wiss had brought with him, said, "How long you figure to stay out at this mine?"

Wycza laughed. "Till it cools," he said.

"Maybe three, four days," Parker told him. "We can stash cars there ahead of time, make our split there."

Chambers, the hillbilly, stretched his long legs out and said, "What's the chance of aerial surveillance? What if the state boys throw heli-copters out?"

"Helicopters," said Paulus.

Edgars said, "There's sheds there, and trees back a ways from the ravine edge. We can all get under cover."

Chambers nodded and scratched his chin. "The truck, too?"

"I'm pretty sure."

Chambers looked at him sideways. "Pretty sure? Pretty sure don't cut it."

"If we can't hide it up top," Edgars told him, "we can always take it down into the ravine. There's an overhang on the south side, we can stick it in under there."

"Just don't like heli-copters."

There was silence then. Parker looked around. Kerwin and Pop Phillips and Salsa hadn't asked anything, but all three of them looked as though they were thinking hard. Parker said, "Everybody in?"

Pop Phillips shook his head. "I'm not quite sure, Parker," he said. "It strikes me as being a pretty ostentatious sort of proposition."

Kerwin said, "How many safes?"

Edgars answered him. "The two bank vaults, the loan company, the three jewelry stores, maybe ten or twelve other stores that'd be worth it."

"How you want to do it, noisy or slow?"

Parker looked at Edgars. "Any people live along Raymond Avenue?"

"No, it's all commercial. There's no homes less than a block away."

"So you want juice," said Kerwin. "That's a hell of a lot of juice to carry around."

Paulus said, "Why not drill? Blow the vaults, but drill the others."

Wiss, the other safe man, said, "Drilling's just as loud, and slower."

"You got a hell of a lot of safes there," Kerwin said.

"But three men doing it," Parker told him. "You hit the payroll, while Paulus and Wiss start on the banks. Then the three of you take the rest of the town."

Kerwin nodded. "Maybe so. You got to blow the vaults, no choice there. But I don't like blowing everything, that's too much juice to carry around."

Paulus said, "Drilling doesn't take long. It might even be, a couple of those safes, all you'll need is a sledge on the combination."

Wiss said, "I don't mind drilling. But you want speed on this job."

Professionals bickering about their speciality; it was taking them away from where they ought to be. Parker said, "You three work it out later. Any way you want to do it is okay."

Elkins, Wiss's partner, said, "What about alarms?"

"What about them?" Edgars asked him. "We'll have the police station sewed up."

"I meant bells. You don't want the main street sounding like New Year's Eve."

"Oh. There aren't any bells."

"None at all?"

"Every business along Raymond Avenue is hooked up to a burglar alarm system at police headquarters. Trip the alarm in one of the banks or a store, and a bell rings in the police station, and a light comes on to show the man on duty where the break is."

Elkins nodded, and said, "That's all right, then."

Salsa spoke up for the first time. He had a trace of accent in his voice. "How soon do you plan to do this?"

"Couple of weeks," Parker told him. "Depends how long it takes to get set."

"What do we do in the meantime?"

"We'll get to that. First, is everybody in? Anybody want to drop out? Phillips?"

Pop Phillips shook his head thoughtfully. "I don't know," he said. "This looks all right to the rest of you, eh? I can't help but feel we're biting off more than we can chew, but if you're all convinced it's feasible, then I imagine that'll have to be good enough for me."

"Only if you're sure," Parker told him.

"That's just his way, Parker," Wycza told him. Phillips had been suggested by Wycza. "If he says he's in, he's in. Right, Pop?"

"I rely on your judgment," Phillips told him. He looked like a rummy night-watchman, baggy pants and all, but sounded like a retired schoolteacher. He'd taken two falls in his lifetime and had done a lot of reading in prison.

"I guess we're all in," said Paulus.

" 'All fools in a circle.' "

"Shut up, Grofield."

"You men give me confidence. This is going to be easier than I thought."

"I only wish Ernie could be here to see this. He *hates* little towns."

"It'll be pleasant, I must admit, to be in uniform once again. I sometimes think I missed my calling."

"More beer?"

They all wanted more beer. When Edgars brought it back and distributed it, Parker got to his feet and said, "We've got some setting up to do. Paulus, you and Wiss ought to take a run out to Copper Canyon and look it over. See if there's any problems we haven't covered."

Wiss said, "I don't like showing my face."

"We'll sell insurance," Paulus told him. "Don't worry, I've done this before. I've got identity cards and brochures and everything. All you do is do a bad job selling insurance, and in between you look around."

Parker said, "If Wiss don't want to, he don't have to. Kerwin?"

Kerwin shrugged. "All right by me."

"Wycza, you and Salsa go out there and take a look at this mining place. But don't stay in Copper Canyon." He turned to Edgars. "What's some other town nearby, bigger than Copper Canyon?"

"Madison."

"All right. Stay in Madison. Chambers, you pick us up a truck, right?"

"I surely will."

"The biggest they make."

"That's the one I'll get, all right."

"Wiss, get together with Paulus and Kerwin before they leave, work up a list of the supplies you need. Then you and Elkins go get the stuff."

Elkins nodded. Wiss said, "Who's handling the cash?"

"Grofield."

"Treasurer and disburser, at your service."

"Littlefield, pick yourself up a car. You and Phillips drive on out there to Madison and start moving groceries out to the mine. Enough for twelve men for a week, just in case. We'll need water, too. Edgars tells me the water there's polluted."

Littlefield said, "Is this the car we'll use in the job?"

"Right. So stay away from Copper Canyon. Arrange with the boys for when any of them wants to bring a car out to stash at the mine, so you can drive them back. The back money pays for your car and the truck and that's it."

Salsa said, "What about the lookout's car? I'm lookout, town line."

"Get yourself a car in town, when we start the operation."

Salsa nodded. "That's good."

Parker told him, "What you want to do right away is pick us up walkie-talkies. Four of them, for you, me, Wycza, and Grofield. Grofield'll be at the telephone company, and he can get in touch with anybody else by phone. Wycza and Elkins will be coming together at the truck all the time, so they only need one walkie-talkie between them."

"Four walkie-talkies," said Salsa. "Very good."

"Buy them here in the East."

Salsa nodded.

Edgars said, "What about me? What do you want me to do?"

Parker shook his head. "Just stay loose. You'll have things to do later."

"Well, what about you? What are you going to do?"

"Guns."

Phillips leaned across the table and said, "Let me have some of that notepaper, will you, Paulus? And does anyone have a pencil? Then we'll make arrangements for rendezvous at the mine, for those of you with cars to leave there."

Wiss said, "Kerwin, Paulus, let's go out in the kitchen and talk."

Littlefield turned to Grofield. "We'll have to work out expenses," he said. "The car, and food, and living expenses."

"No living expenses," Grofield told him. "We shaved that much out already."

Littlefield pursed his lips. "If you think it works better that way."

Grofield grinned at him. "You want me to go get some more? And you pay it back double, so that way you pay your living expenses twice."

"That's the way my income tax will read," Littlefield told him.

"Income tax?" Grofield stared at him. "You pay income tax?"

"On every penny."

"I bet *your* return shakes them up."

"I account for every penny of income," Littlefield told him, "but I am forced, of course, to invent my sources."

"Why bother?"

Littlefield leaned closer to him. "You're a young man, you can still learn. Pay attention to this. You can steal in this country, you can rape and murder, you can bribe public officials, you can pollute the morals of the young, you can burn your place of business down for the insurance money, you can do almost anything you want, and if you act with just a little caution and common sense you'll never even be indicted. But if you don't pay your income tax, Grofield, you will go to jail."

"Oh sure," said Grofield. "Sure thing."

"Parker knows I'm right. You pay tax, don't you, Parker?"

Parker nodded. Under the Charles Willis name he owned

pieces of a few losing businesses here and there, and they gave him the background to cover his income on his tax return.

Grofield shook his head. "I don't get it. You're putting me on."

"Income taxes is federal," Parker told him.

"So's a bank, for Christ's sake."

"I don't mean federal offense, I mean federal, whose money it is. A bank is stockholders, but income tax is government money."

Pop Phillips said, "Those are words of wisdom, Grofield. I only fell twice, and once it was income tax. I got three years, and I'm still paying the back taxes. Why do you think I'm not retired?"

"I'll put you onto my accountant," Littlefield said. "He'll get you straightened out."

Grofield got to his feet, looking agitated. "That's a lot of crap. Don't talk to me about that. Income tax!"

Littlefield shrugged. "You'll go to jail," he said.

Parker saw Grofield getting mad, and said, "Back to business. We got a lot to set up tonight."

3

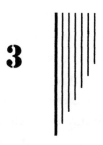

"Machine guns," said the blind man. "They're expensive, machine guns."

"I know," said Parker.

"And hard to come by."

"I know."

"The government tries to keep tabs on them. It's tough to find one without a history."

"I need three. And three rifles. And eight handguns."

"Rifles, handguns," said the blind man. "No problem. Machine guns, that's a problem."

Parker shook his head in irritation, though the blind man couldn't see it. He'd come to the blind man because he was the one to talk to if you wanted machine guns. Parker would have preferred to go to Amos Klee, in Syracuse, but Klee was only good on handguns. It was the blind man, called Scofe, who should be able to supply the machine guns.

Parker said, "You don't have them? You can't get them?"

"Sit," said the blind man. "Sit, sit. Let me think."

Parker sat, and let him think.

They were in the filthy back room of a cluttered hobby shop on Second Avenue in Albany, New York. Scofe owned the hobby shop, and it was run by a sloppy woman with red hair who didn't trust anybody. The filth and the clutter and Scofe's blindness and the woman's surliness combined to keep customers at a minimum. Scofe didn't need much to support himself anyway and he got most of his income from guns. He was good with his hands, could disassemble and reassemble a rifle faster than most men with eyes, and was even a good shot. He fired at sound targets, a small bell hung up in a breeze or—his favorite kind of target—a child's toy of the click-click type.

Scofe scratched his chin. He hadn't shaved for a few days, and his fingernails made a harsh dry sound against his beard stubble. He said, "Shotgun no good? I got good shotguns, sawed-off or what you want."

"Machine guns. Three."

"You know what the Germans call a machine gun? *Kugelspritz*. Bullet squirter. All noise, no accuracy."

"Three."

Scofe shrugged, and made a motion as though washing his hands. "Not my affair. I got a Schmeisser, a burp gun. Old, but in good condition."

"That's one."

Scofe chuckled, his shoulders rising and falling. "Parker,"

he said. "Parker, Parker. I hear you got a new face, but your voice don't change, or your style. You don't like me, do you, Parker?"

"I don't give a damn about you."

"You don't like the dirty old blind man. He smells bad. Yah. Parker?"

"Maybe I'll go to Amos Klee."

"For machine guns? No, Parker. For machine guns, you come to Scofe. You want the burp gun?"

"Let me see it."

Scofe pointed. "Over there you see a shelf. Long boxes on it, battleship models. Bottom box, second from the left. Bring it here."

Parker got the box. The ones he had to move were light, but the one he wanted was heavy. He started to open it and Scofe said, "I'll open it, Parker. Bring it here."

Parker brought it over to him. Scofe was sitting in a squeaky kitchen chair next to a table, an old scarred work-table with nothing on it. Parker handed him the box and Scofe put it on the table, half turned to be closer to the table, and took the top off the box. It was full of parts. Scofe's hands touched the parts, his long fingers moving like worms in a garden. Parker watched him as he put the parts together, feeling in the bottom of the box for screws, using a small metal screwdriver he took from his hip pocket. He put the parts together and when he was done there was a burp gun on the table. "There," he said. "You like it?"

Parker picked it up. There was rust on it, a little, not

much. It was an old gun, but it looked to be in good shape. The places where it was rusted were where identification marks had been filed away, leaving the metal rough.

"Well?"

"How much."

"I don't haggle, Parker, you know I never haggle."

"How much?"

"One twenty-five."

Parker put the gun back down on the table. "What else you got?"

Scofe chuckled again. His hands reached out and found the gun and he disassembled it again, putting everything back in the model battleship box. When he was finished, he put the top on the box again and said, "You want to put it back? You're not interested?"

"Leave it out awhile. What else you got?"

"You take the burp, I can let you have two tommys, a hundred apiece."

"Where are they?"

"You know me, Parker, they aren't bad guns. I don't touch bad guns."

Parker knew that, but he wanted to see them before making up his mind. He said, "You know me. I always look first."

"I never look first, Parker. The smelly old blind man never looks at all." He swiveled around and pointed to a corner. "Road-racer sets there," he said. "Big square boxes. Fourth and fifth down. They're all assembled."

Parker went over. The fourth and fifth boxes were heavier

than the first three. Parker felt the sixth box, and it was heavy, too. He carried the fourth and fifth over to the table, opened them, and looked at two Thompson .45 submachine guns, each equipped with a twenty-shot clip. They both looked all right. He put the tops back on the boxes and said, "These are good. I'll take three of these."

"Those two are all I got."

"Then I want a road-racer set. The sixth from the top."

"You're a bastard, Parker. You're a rotten bastard. You're a filthy rotten son of a bitch. You take advantage of a poor old blind man, you'd spit on your own mother. You're a cesspool, a walking cesspool, you're vomit, you're a cheap two-bit rotten punk."

"Shut up, Scofe."

Scofe shut up. He stuck his right hand up to his face and gnawed on a knuckle. He looked like an old squirrel.

Parker said, "One hundred each for three tommys."

"Two tommys. And one twenty-five for the burp."

"I don't want the burp."

"Then one-fifty each for the tommys."

"Good-bye, Scofe."

"I don't haggle, Parker, you know me."

Parker turned away and started for the front of the store. He opened the door and went through, leaving the door open behind him, and walked down between the display cases. The sullen woman watched him suspiciously.

Parker got halfway to the street door and then Scofe called, "Parker! Hey! Come back here!"

Parker turned around and went back. The woman kept watching him. He went into the back room again and said, "What?"

"Put these boxes away. You can't leave these boxes out."

"I'm going to see Amos Klee."

"You're a liar."

"He can get me guns. I wait a few days, that's all. He'll scout around for me."

Scofe twisted his head back and forth. "If I could *see* you!"

"It's all in my voice, Scofe."

"I hate you like poison. Like poison."

"I don't like to deal with you, Scofe. You smell bad. What's your price, the three tommys?"

"Three-fifty. That's it, that's the lowest."

"Deal."

"Tell my woman to come in here."

Parker went to the door and motioned to the woman. "Come in here."

She came in, and Scofe said, "Every transaction cash. This transaction, you pay the cash, then we see what else you want."

The woman said, "How much?"

"Three-fifty. For three road racers."

Parker took an envelope out of his jacket pocket, and counted three hundred and fifty dollars onto the table, while the woman watched. When he was done, she said, "Okay."

"You're all right, Parker." Scofe raised his head and smiled. He was filthy, and his eyes were covered by a white film, and his teeth were brown. When he smiled, he looked like a parody of something unspeakable. "You're all right," he said again. "You don't mean all those things you say to me."

Parker went over and got the sixth heavy road-racer box. He put it with the first two, and picked up all three. He said to the woman, "Come out with me and open the car door."

Scofe said, "What about the other stuff you wanted?"

"Never mind."

"You're going to Klee?"

Parker ignored him. He said to the woman, "Come on," and started for the front of the store.

"You scum! You vomit! You stinking cesspool!"

Parker walked through the store to the street, the woman coming behind him. She opened the rear door of the car, and Parker put the three boxes on the seat. He closed the door and nodded to the woman. She said, "He's getting worse."

Parker hadn't expected her to talk. He stopped and looked at her and said, "He's stupid. There's others in the same business."

"He don't get half the business he used to. You, too, you're going somewhere else now."

"Tell him, not me."

"It's because he's blind."

"He ought to be used to it by now."

Parker went around and got behind the wheel. It was a one-year-old Mercury, painted blue and white, a mace he'd picked up yesterday in Harrisburg, Pennsylvania. He'd drive it out to North Dakota, stash it at the mine, and drive away in it after the job. Then he'd get rid of it. The Pennsylvania plate and registration paper looked good enough if he stayed out of Pennsylvania. From the little mileage on it, he thought it had probably been taken right from a dealer. Even with planned obsolescence, it would last as long as he'd need it.

He made a U-turn on Second Avenue and went up the hill and over to the Thruway entrance. The way he'd originally figured, he'd go back to Jersey City and stay over tonight, then pick up Edgars in the morning and head west. But now, having to stop off in Syracuse to see Klee, he'd have to make better time than that, get Edgars to leave tonight. If everything worked out, they could maybe pull it next Thursday night.

He picked up the ticket at the Thruway entrance and headed south. He was impatient, but he stayed just under the speed limit. He didn't want a trooper looking into the road-racer boxes on the backseat.

4

"This is Jean," said Edgars. He seemed uncomfortable.

Jean wasn't uncomfortable at all. She was a hard-looking blonde of about thirty, short, with hard, conical breasts. She was sitting on the sofa in the living room of Edgars' apartment, her legs crossed and skirt hiked up to show her tan.

Parker looked at Jean and then at Edgars. He said, "So what?"

Edgars swallowed. "She's coming along," he said.

"Since when?"

"Since always. She's always been with me."

"Always?" Parker looked at her. She wouldn't be with anybody always, and especially not Edgars.

"She doesn't have anything to do with the business arrangement," Edgars said. "I always had her go out to a movie or something when we had a meeting. And she can wait for us in Madison or somewhere until we're done."

Jean smiled lazily, looking at Parker like a nightclub booker at an audition, waiting for the new act to do something interesting. She said, "I'll get along."

Parker looked at Edgars and shook his head. "No dice. She can wait for you here."

"Why? She'll keep out of the way, I guarantee it."

"She'll keep out of the way better in Jersey City."

"Parker, I give you my word—"

"I don't want your word."

Jean said, "Who's the boss around here, anyway, honey?"

"Nobody," Parker told her. "And that's just the kind of trouble you bring with you." He turned to Edgars. "She stays here."

Edgars was embarrassed and uneasy. He felt like a fool, in front of the woman. He said, "Nobody else will even *see* her. I guarantee it. We'll take her partway and leave her in Madison or somewhere. I'll never say a word to any of the others; they won't even know she exists."

Jean laughed and said, "Just a quiet little mouse, that's me. Quiet little mouse."

Parker said, "She'll show up in the middle of it. At the town, or the hideout."

Edgars shook his head. "No, she won't, Parker. I'm not a professional at this kind of thing, like you, but I know better than that. She doesn't know where the job *is*, except North Dakota, and she doesn't know where the hideout is either."

"Except North Dakota," said Jean, and laughed again. She

looked at Parker, a challenge in her eyes, and said, "You don't have to worry about me, Parker. I know my business, too."

"We leave her farther away than Madison," Parker said. He didn't like giving in on this thing, but looking at Edgars he saw he would have to. The trouble the woman could cause if they took her along was less than the trouble Edgars could cause, lousing up the operation out of pique and embarrassment, if they didn't take her along. "We leave her in some town this side of the North Dakota line."

"*I* pick the town," she said.

Edgars nodded, grateful for the compromise. "All right," he said. "I understand what you mean, Parker. That's why I kept her out of sight all the time."

"Sometimes I feel like a sheep or something," she said. "Couldn't you bastards at least lower your voices? You talk about me like I'm not even here, and I'm getting irritated."

They both ignored her. Parker said to Edgars, "I got to make a stop in Syracuse, so we'll have to leave tonight."

"Tonight? I'm not packed or anything."

"So pack."

Jean said, "What about me? Half my stuff's still over to the old place."

Edgars wanted to hold on to her, but he knew she was a liability. He sounded irritated when he said, "So go over to the old place and *get* your stuff."

"Jesus," she said. "It's like the army. Alert! Alert! Alert! Pack your bag in the middle of the night and run your ass off."

"I told you before about that language."

"Up yours," she said.

Parker said, "Argue later. Right now, pack."

She turned to Parker, saying, "Drive me over to the old place."

"Take a cab."

"*You're* the one in the hurry, ugly."

"You better take her," Edgars said. "Otherwise, she'll be gone for hours. I'd take her, but I got to pack. And I don't have a car." He said the last with surprise.

Parker was about ready to tell them both to go to hell, but then he thought of Edgars and his private reasons. The bitch might know something about them. He said, "All right, let's go."

"Be right back, honey." She twisted the last word like a knife.

They left the building and got into the Mercury, and Parker said, "Where to?"

"Just straight ahead awhile. I'll show you where to turn. Don't worry, ugly, you won't get lost with me."

"I know."

They rode four blocks in silence, and then she told him to turn right. It was after eleven at night, the middle of the week, and not much traffic on the streets. Parker drove along steadily, trying to think of a way to lead in to the questions he wanted to ask. Being no good at small talk was sometimes a disadvantage.

Ahead of him, a traffic light switched to red. He stopped

and waited, and no cars came along from right or left to take advantage of the green light.

She said, "What do you know about him?"

Was she going to volunteer it all herself? He said, "Edgars, you mean?"

"Who else? What kind of a bird is he?"

So that took care of that. She knew less about Edgars than Parker did. On the off chance, he said, "I thought you knew him from always."

She laughed. "That's his story. On my side, 'always' looks like three weeks."

"Since he came to town."

"I guess."

"You didn't sound like North Dakota."

"Compliments yet."

"That wasn't a compliment."

The light changed again, and he drove on. Two blocks farther on she told him to make a left. Her voice was cold as ice. He got stopped by another traffic light, went two more blocks and she said, "Just ahead on the right."

There was a fireplug handy. He parked next to it. She said, "You want a ticket?"

"What do you care?"

"Not a thing, ugly. Wait here, I'll be as quick as I can."

"I'll come along."

"Why?"

"So you'll be quicker."

"Mister Edgars has such sweet friends."

It was a brick apartment building, the entrance flanked by coachlamps bearing twenty-five-watt bulbs. There was a small green elevator, which took them slowly to the third floor. As they walked down the hall, she rummaged in her purse for a key and said, "If my roomie's in, try not to be any uglier than you have to."

She unlocked a door and pushed it open. The apartment was dark. She felt along the wall and found the light switch. It was a ceiling light that came on, showing a large room full of clutter. Newspapers, magazines, paperback books, scattered all over the place. A studio couch was covered by wrinkled sheets and blankets; a pillow was on the floor next to it. There were wicker chairs and end tables and two lamps. A gray carpet was on the floor.

"My roomie's a mess. Come in, if you're coming. Shut the door. You want a drink?"

"No. Just pack."

"I'm going to love traveling with you, ugly. You mind if I take a shower?"

"Yes."

"Tough. That's just plain tough."

"If you want to know how far you can push me," he told her, "you can find out right now."

She hesitated, and then she shrugged. "I don't care. You didn't want me to come along, you talked about me like I wasn't there, so I got sore. What do you expect?"

"I didn't expect you at all."

"Well, I'm here. I'll keep out of the way like a good girl,

and I won't make trouble with Edgars or anybody else. All right?"

Parker shrugged. "That's all I ask."

"So I'll take a very quick shower. Quickest ever, I promise. Okay?"

Parker looked at his watch. "We want to be out of here in twenty minutes."

"Fifteen. Okay?"

She was making an effort, so he ought to make an effort, too. He made an effort, relaxed his face a little, and said, "Okay."

"There's booze in the kitchen, if you want a drink. And I won't call you ugly anymore. Okay?"

Now she was overdoing it. "Just get moving," he said.

"You're hard to get along with, you know that?"

He didn't say anything at all to that, so after a minute she went on into the other room. Parker found the kitchen, found a bottle of Philadelphia and a glass and a tray of ice cubes, and made himself a drink. He could hear the shower running.

She was available. Some other time, he'd probably do something about it, but not now. He ran to a pattern that way; right after a job he was raring, he couldn't get enough. Then it would slacken off, gradually, over months, until he didn't give a damn at all. When he was working, he was an acetic, not out of choice but just because that's the way he was built.

He stood in the kitchen doorway, looking at the messy living room and pulling at his drink. He heard the shower stop, and then she called, "You get a drink?"

"Yes."

"Make me one?"

He went back to the kitchen and made her one, just whisky over ice in a glass. He carried the two glasses across the living room and into a small airless bedroom with a closed venetian blind over the one window. She was wearing a white terry-cloth robe, and a suitcase was open on the double bed. Her hair was wet, plastered to her head, and her face was scrubbed clean of makeup. That way she looked younger and less hard. Without the shrill good looks that cosmetics gave her, she had a plain and somewhat thin face.

"Just put it on the dresser," she said. "You want to dry my back?"

"You do it." He turned away.

"Wait a second."

"Why?"

She was studying him with confusion. "You a good friend of Edgars, or what?"

"What," he said.

"You always in such a goddam hurry like this?"

"I am this time."

"I try to be friendly, and you put me down. What's the matter with you?"

They were going to be traveling halfway across the country together, and she could always louse up Edgars' effectiveness in the operation some way if she wanted to, so he made the effort again and said, "Maybe it'll be different afterwards."

"Afterwards what? You mean after this big secret mission you and charming Billy got on?"

"That's right."

She shrugged. "Okay, I'll dry my own back. It wouldn't stay wet till then, anyway."

Parker went back to the living room, tipped a wicker chair forward to dump newspapers and magazines out of it onto the floor, and sat down. He looked at his watch; six minutes had gone by.

When she came out, dressed in black skirt and white blouse and tan summer coat, carrying a suitcase in each hand, he looked at his watch again. Exactly fifteen minutes. She said, "Well? Do I get the gold star?"

"Yeah."

"Sure. Gold-star mother. I had a boy in the service, but he died. Here, you're the gentleman, carry these things. I'll be right back." She put the suitcases down and went into the kitchen. She came back carrying the bottle.

5

"There's the turnoff," Edgars said. He pointed.

Parker turned the Mercury off the highway and onto the secondary road. The highway had been concrete, three lanes wide, straight as a bowling alley. The secondary road was blacktop, two lanes wide, and curved a lot. But the road surface was good, they could still make good time.

In the trunk of the car, along with the three road-racer sets from Scofe, were three rifles and eight pistols from Amos Klee. The rifles were a Higgins Model 45, chambered for .30-30, a Ruger .44 carbine, and a Winchester Standard 70, chambered for .30-06. The pistols were mostly S&W, .32 or .38 revolvers. Two boxes on the floor behind the front seat contained ammunition.

Yesterday they'd left the blonde, Jean, in a motel outside Thief River Falls, Minnesota. The name of the city struck Edgars as funny, which is why they picked it. Edgars wrote down the motel phone number, so he could call her from time to time and let her know everything was all right.

One way or another, she'd apparently made up her mind about Parker the first night, back in Jersey City. On the trip out she kept to herself, saying little, sitting on the backseat with her feet on the ammunition boxes, working her way through bottle after bottle. Every time they stopped, Edgars had to go buy her another bottle. "Gold-star mother," she said to Parker once, and started to cry. But she cried silently and didn't bother him. She was only about thirty, so the gold-star mother stuff was crap. Probably meant a boyfriend killed in the army. Every tramp has an excuse.

But yesterday they'd unloaded her at Thief River Falls. Edgars gave her a bottle and some money, and promised to call every other day. Then he and Parker drove the last stretch to North Dakota. At Madison they picked up the highway that connected with 22A, the road into Copper Canyon. Three miles this side of it they came to the secondary road that headed toward the abandoned strip mine.

Parker glanced at the speedometer. "You said six miles to the dirt road?"

"About that."

They rode in silence, till Edgars said, "There it is."

Parker looked again at the speedometer. Six point two. He nodded, and made the turn.

The dirt road was in worse condition than the blacktop road; it hadn't been kept up since the mining company had moved on. Parker kept it at thirty, and the car jounced badly, but never badly enough to force him to slow down. He checked the rear-view mirror from time to time, but the land here was clay or something and there was practically no dust raised in their wake. That was good.

They ran through a small wood that was choked with underbrush and then they emerged suddenly on a brown flat plain. Just ahead were squat small buildings, some of corrugated metal, some of wood siding. There was a station wagon parked up close to one of the wooden buildings. As Parker drove the Mercury closer a man came into view, walking leisurely toward them. It was Littlefield.

Parker braked to a halt, and Littlefield came around to his side and said, "You made good time. How you like it here?"

"Where do I put the car?"

Littlefield pointed. "That one over there. We ripped some of the wall down on the other side, so we could get cars in."

Parker nodded, and drove forward again. Seen up close, the buildings were just sheds, each with a single door and one or two windows in each wall. Parker made a circle past the shed Littlefield had pointed out, and swung around to face it. It was one of the corrugated ones, and a couple of pieces of the wall were lying on the ground to one side. Parker drove through the open space and stopped.

There was just a dirt floor inside, and darkness, and dry heat. Parker felt sweat breaking out on his face before he was out of the car. There was a Plymouth already in there; with Parker's Mercury added the shed was full.

"Christ," said Edgars. "Hot."

They went back out to the sunlight and walked around the shed and over to Littlefield, who was standing next to the station wagon, watching them. Littlefield was wearing gray work pants and a flannel shirt and a cowboy hat. He didn't look like a member of the board of directors anymore; out here he looked like a hanging judge.

Littlefield said, "We set this one up for living quarters. You go on in, I'll stay out here and watch for them."

"Better get the wagon out of sight."

"One car don't make any difference."

"Get it out of sight anyway."

Littlefield pursed his lips and went away to get the car out of sight.

Parker and Edgars went into the wooden shed. Inside, it was one large room, and it seemed a little cooler than outside. Folded army cots were stacked in a corner near some cardboard cartons. A folding table and some folding chairs were set up in the middle of the room.

Five men were in the room. Kerwin and Wycza and Salsa and Pop Phillips were sitting around the table, playing poker. Paulus was in the corner, inventorying the contents of the cartons.

Phillips waved a greeting. "Welcome to our happy home," he said.

Edgars said, "It looks okay, doesn't it?"

"It's okay," Parker told him. But he felt exposed, these little sheds on the flat brown plain.

Phillips said, "It was a deal of work for two old men, I'll

tell you that. Me and Littlefield, we took down some walls to make garages, we transported food, we buried jugs of water under one of the sheds, we swept up, hung some curtains, planted azaleas outside the windows, and hired a butler."

"It looks good," Parker said. He looked at Kerwin. "How's the town?"

"Easy."

"Can we do it this week?"

"Sure."

"No problems?"

"None."

"Of course," Pop Phillips said, "Wycza and Salsa, here, they did help a bit. But for two old codgers, Littlefield and me, we did our share."

"Sure you did," Wycza told him. Wycza always seemed proud of Phillips, as though he'd invented him.

Paulus, from the corner, said, "I'm not sure we've got enough food."

"We've got enough," Phillips told him. "We've got plenty, don't you worry."

Littlefield stuck his head in the doorway. "Somebody coming." He went away again.

Parker went over to a window and watched a green Ford coming closer. It stopped. Littlefield went over to talk to the driver and then pointed. The car moved again. When it went by, Parker saw it was Wiss and Elkins.

Salsa came over. "I got the walkie-talkies. Shall I explain them to you?"

"Sure."

They went over to where the walkie-talkies were, nesting in four boxes like outsize shoe boxes. Salsa explained they were a matched set, he'd had them fixed for him. Talk into any one and the voice came out of all the other three. You couldn't talk to just one of the other walkie-talkies, but you couldn't talk to any walkie-talkies except these three, either. "I told the man we were a group of hunters," he said. He smiled, and his teeth were white and even. The Latin lover, with a tan. "I told the truth," he said. "We are a group of hunters."

"They look good," Parker told him. "Good work."

Wiss and Elkins came in then, and Wiss said to Phillips, "I need a cool place to keep the juice. Littlefield says to talk to you."

"One second." Phillips looked at his cards, said, "Fold," and got to his feet. "I'll show you. Sit in for me, Elkins."

Elkins sat down at the table, and Wiss and Phillips left. Salsa, still standing beside Parker, said, "This Thursday?"

"Right."

"Three days. Good. Three days before, four days after. One week is about all I will be able to take of this place."

Parker nodded. Their original plan had been to stay in towns around the general area until the night of the raid, but they'd decided instead to gather here today, and stay until after the job was finished. This way there wouldn't be any strangers in nearby towns for the locals to remember later.

Edgars came over and said, "We're set, huh? This is like I told you, isn't it?"

"It's fine. When Phillips comes back, have him show you some place to stow the ammunition. That shed's too hot."

"Will do."

Littlefield stuck his head in again. "Chambers coming."

Parker followed him outside and watched. Chambers was wrestling the truck across the uneven ground, and the trailer, empty, was jogging back and forth. The cab was a Mack, painted red, and the trailer a metal-color Fruehauf, just about the biggest standard size made. Neither cab nor trailer had any sort of company name or markings visible on them.

Parker stuck his head back in the door and called, "Edgars! Where's the road down into the ravine?"

Edgars came outside and pointed. "Down past those sheds. You see the dropoff?"

"All right."

Chambers had pulled the truck to a stop near the shed. Parker went over and climbed up into the cab and shut the door. Chambers was grinning, his face dirty, streaked with sweat. "This is a big old bastard," he said.

"How was the road, coming in?"

"Not too bad. Couldn't top thirty-five, but I got no load. When we come back with the ass full of men and gold, she'll sit just fine on that road. You got a cigarette?"

Parker gave him a cigarette and lit one for himself. Chambers said, "I got it offen Chemy. He says to tell you hello, and his brother run that woman off. That make sense to you?"

"Yeah. Edgars says the road down to the bottom's over that way. Let's see if this truck'll do it."

"If it don't, we can sing hymns while we fall."

Chambers started the truck forward again, slowly, and after a minute Parker could see the edge. The brown earth just stopped, and there was midair. Across the way, a good distance off, the earth started again; over there he could see the sheer brown wall going downward.

"Son of a bitch," said Chambers. "I bet that's it there." He pointed out the cab window.

Chambers stopped the truck, and they both got down and walked over to look at the road. Down below, eighty feet down, there was a flat brown expanse with nothing growing on it. Two streams of red water angled and wandered through it. It looked like a sunny part of Hell.

"Look at that," said Chambers. "Red water. What do you think, maybe it's wine."

"There's the road."

They both looked at it. It ran down the side of the wall, one lane wide, a dirt road with two broad ruts running down it. It went down at a steep slope, but it was straight all the way, reaching bottom at the far end of the ravine, where the ravine sloped up somewhat. The ruts circled there and came back along the ravine floor.

"I don't know," said Chambers. "I don't like the looks of it."

"Ore trucks did it."

"They're built low to the ground. Low center of gravity. I got me an empty trailer on there."

"It's straight. Just take it slow, that's all."

"Come on along, Parker. It's your idea."

They went back and got into the cab again. Chambers released the brake and eased the truck forward to the edge and slowly down the incline. They could hear the trailer couplings banging.

"She wants to run," said Chambers. "She wants to fly down this goddam road."

"You'll make it," Parker told him. "No problem."

"Sure."

The truck inched down the wall to the bottom, and Chambers swung the wheel to bring it around facing the other way. He stopped it, shifted into neutral, and said, "Give me another cigarette."

They smoked a minute in silence, Chambers wiping sweat off his face onto his sleeve, and then Parker said, "Looks like they cut into the wall over there. Let's go over and look."

"I shoulda got me a biddy panel truck."

Chambers wrestled the truck forward, and they came to a part where the side of the ravine angled inward sharply from top to bottom, leaving a narrow strip of the bottom in shadow. Chambers backed and filled till he got the truck in close to the side, in the shadow, and then they both got out and looked at it. Parker said, "We want to get some black paint. That metal shines too much."

"Brown paint. Make it blend right in. Camio-flage."

"All right, brown."

"Now we walk up, right?"

"Right."

"Christ. I'd be better off working."

"Come on."

Chambers took a step, stopped, and said, "Rotten eggs. Smell it?"

"That's your wine rivers. Sulphur."

"Real homey place."

They walked back up the road to the top and went into the shed where the others were. Grofield was there now, making everybody present. Parker looked at him and waited for him to say, "All fools in a circle."

But what he said was, " 'Come, Watson, come! The game is afoot!!' "

"This isn't summer stock."

"Good old Parker. This Thursday, huh?"

"This Thursday." He turned to Littlefield. "All the cars stashed?"

"Right. Six of them. Two each in three sheds."

"We better put the sides back on, in case anybody comes out here. What about the wagon?"

"I put it down in the woods, off the road."

"Good."

Parker and Wycza and Salsa and Grofield went out and put the torn-down sections of wall back into place, hiding the cars inside. Two men would be leaving in each car, after the job, each car going off to a different destination. Wiss and Elkins would leave together, and Wycza and Phillips, Paulus and Littlefield, Chambers and Salsa, Grofield and Kerwin. Parker would take Edgars with him, pick up the blonde at Thief River Falls, and drive them as far as Chicago. After that, they were on their own; Chicago was where Parker would dump the Mercury.

After they got the walls back up, and returned to the living-in shed, Parker found Littlefield and said, "One last trip to town for you. We need brown paint, to cover the truck."

"Right. What if I go in after dark?"

"If you can find a store open."

"There's a hardware store I seen open nights in Madison."

"Good."

Parker dragged a couple of food cartons over to the table and sat down on them. "Deal me in," he said. Behind him, Grofield was reciting, playing Falstaff and Hal both, *Henry IV, Part I*, Act 1, Scene 2.

6

Chambers brought the truck up at eleven-thirty, using the parking lights only. The rest were waiting for him in the darkness at the top. In the last three days, they hadn't seen a single stranger, afoot or in a car or even in a plane. They might as well have been the last people on earth.

Parker and Salsa and Edgars carried machine guns—Parker had discovered, to his surprise, that Edgars already knew how to operate a tommy—and Grofield, Chambers, and Littlefield carried rifles. Salsa and Parker both also wore pistols, as did Kerwin and Phillips and Paulus and Wycza and Wiss and Elkins. Parker and Salsa and Wycza and Grofield had walkie-talkies strapped to their backs.

Chambers was to drive the truck, Littlefield the station wagon. Phillips and Edgars and Grofield were to ride in the wagon, the rest in the truck.

Chambers cut the parking lights as soon as he stopped the

truck. There was no moon, but the sky was clear and full of stars. There was enough vague light to see by, sufficient for everyone to board.

Six men climbed into the back of the truck and sat along the sides, bracing themselves for the bumpy ride to come. Paulus and Wycza and Kerwin on one side, Wiss and Elkins and Salsa on the other. The safe men's equipment was to ride in the station wagon, where it would get a less bumpy trip.

Parker went over to the station wagon and said to Little-field, "Remember, give us five minutes. We'll run slower than you, you can catch up when we get to town."

"Right."

"Don't catch up before we pass the trooper barracks."

"I remember, Parker."

"See you later."

Parker went back to the truck, took off his walkie-talkie, and climbed up into the cab with Chambers. He put the walkie-talkie on the floor between his legs and said, "All set."

Chambers put on his parking lights again, and the truck jolted forward.

It was seven miles to the secondary road, and they did it at a crawl, not because of the bumps but because of the bad visibility. Chambers leaned far over the wheel, peering out through the windshield at the dimly seen dirt road. Beside him, Parker lit a cigarette and sat quiet. The last few minutes before a job, he was always quiet, almost in suspended animation. He had no imagination for the few hours ahead, nor worry, nor anticipation, nor anything else. His consciousness worked at the level of recording the jouncing of the truck cab and the feel of the cigarette smoke and the darkness beyond the windshield.

They got to the secondary road and made their turn, and Chambers sighed. He sat back more comfortably, switched on his headlights, and the truck picked up speed. After a minute, Chambers said, "You ever get scared, times like this, Parker?"

Parker roused himself, and said, "No."

"You're lucky. I could use me a jolt of store-bought blended right about now." He laughed, a little shakily. "If them streams would of been wine," he said, "they'd be dry right now. You know, I can smell sulphur in this cab? This here's a good road, they'll be no problem coming back. Be light then, too."

Chambers talked on, working off nervous energy, and Parker sat silent beside him. They made the six miles to the highway and turned left. Up to now they hadn't seen any other traffic, but a mile along the highway they saw headlights in front of them. They came on, moving fast, and a foreign sports car raced by, looking to them in the cab of the truck so low and small it could have gone under the truck instead of next to it.

"Maybe I'll buy me one of them," said Chambers.

Parker leaned forward a little bit and looked at the rearview mirror outside the right window. A way back, he could see headlights. "If that's Littlefield," he said, "I'll crack his skull."

"Don't worry 'bout Littlefield. He knows what he's doing."

By the time they made the turnoff on to 22A, the headlights had dropped farther back. They rolled along, right on the speed limit, and after they passed the trooper barracks—a squat brick building with yellow lights behind the windows, off to their left, surrounded by flat emptiness—Parker said, "Slow down a little now. Give Littlefield a chance to catch up." The headlights of the station wagon were much farther back now, almost invisible.

Ahead of them, on the right, was a sign. They came closer and the truck lights illuminated it:

WELCOME

to

COPPER CANYON

"Son of a gun," said Chambers. "Son of a gun."

THREE

1

Officers Felder and Mason were on night duty in Copper Canyon's only patrol car. They rode along in companionable silence, looking for but not expecting to see violators of the city curfew. It was just a few minutes after midnight, and here and there lights were still on behind windows, but the sidewalks were empty. The radio hissed like coffee brewing; at the other end, Officer Nieman had nothing to say.

The prowl car was a Ford, two years old, painted light green and white, with *Police* written in large letters on the doors and hood and trunk. The dashboard lights were green, and there was a small red dot of light, like a ruby, on the radio. Officer Mason wanted a cigarette but couldn't have one, because Officer Felder, who was driving, was allergic to cigarette smoke. Officer Mason said, "What say we take a break? I could use a smoke."

"Let me swing down around by the west gate. George is on there tonight."

"Fine by me."

They were on Blake Street, east of Raymond Avenue. Officer Felder drove over to Raymond Avenue and turned right, and the west gate to the refinery was six blocks dead ahead.

A few cars were parked along Raymond Avenue, as usual. Between Loomis and Orange Streets, against the right-hand curb, there was a huge tractor trailer parked. It was brown, all over brown. Officer Mason looked at it and thought to himself, *Funny color for a truck.*

He reached into his pocket and pulled out a pack of cigarettes. He got one out, then got his lighter out. He was ready.

They were almost to the gate when the hissing radio suddenly spoke. "Officer Felder, Officer Mason. Officer Felder, Officer Mason."

Officer Mason looked at it in surprise. What the hell kind of way to talk was that? They were first-name basis, always. What the hell was this all about?

He grinned and said to Officer Felder, "Old Fred's gettin' highfalutin."

"He's just kidding around."

Officer Mason picked up the microphone and said, "Yes, *sir*, Officer Nieman, what can I do for you, sir?"

"Come on into the station. Something's come up."

"What's come up?"

"Just get in here. Make it fast."

There was something funny in Officer Nieman's voice,

some sort of agitation. Officer Mason said, "Okay, Fred, here we come." He hung up the microphone again and said to Officer Felder, "*Some*thing's sure got him upset. You hear his voice?"

"I heard it." Officer Felder had already made the turn into Caulkins Street, and was driving toward police headquarters.

"That's a funny thing," said Officer Mason.

"What is?"

"Kidding around one minute, then all upset the next."

"Maybe he wasn't kidding around. Maybe he got all formal and everything because he was upset already. Got rattled or something."

"Well, let's see what it is."

The police station was a modern building. It, and the fire department building across the street, had both been built five years ago, both with the same architect. They were built of tan brick, broad low buildings one story high, very similar in appearance except for the wide garage-type doors across half of the fire department building façade. Flanking the police station entrance were large modernistic faceted green lights, and across the street the fire department entrance was flanked by similar lights in red.

Officer Felder pulled to the curb in front of the building, in the No Parking zone, one of the few in town. They both got out of the car and went up the cement walk past the well-tended lawn into the building. They entered upon a hallway, and the Command Room—as the architect had called it—where Fred Nieman would be, was to the left. It was a large room, with desks along one wall, and a counter in front of the area where the radio and booking desk were located.

They went into the Command Room, and Fred Nieman looked at them from over by the radio. He didn't stand up or say anything or do anything. He offered them a weak and sheepish smile, and just sat there.

A voice behind them said, quietly, "There's seven guns on you. Either of you make a single solitary move, you're dead seven times."

The two officers froze. Both of them thought immediately that it was some sort of gag, and both looked at Officer Nieman to find a clue in his face. But Nieman's face was pale and frightened and sheepish, slit by a nervous, ashamed smile.

Footsteps sounded on the black composition flooring, coming from behind them, going to right and to left. Two men came around in front of them, both in dark work clothing, both wearing black hoods, slit three times for eyes and mouth. One of the two was carrying a Thompson submachine gun and had what looked like a walkie-talkie strapped to his back. The other one had a walkie-talkie, too, and carried a rifle.

Mason thought, *A war attack. Commies!* But even while he was thinking it, he knew that wasn't it. This was something else. It might even be something worse.

Another black-hooded man, this one with a rifle but no walkie-talkie, stood up from where he'd been crouched beside the radio, out of sight from the door, and said, "Okay, Fred boy, git on over there by your pals."

Officer Nieman got shakily to his feet and went around the

end of the counter and came across the floor toward Mason and Felder. His face was pale, and shone with sweat under the fluorescent lights. A look of apology and shame was all over his face. Mason, watching him, thought Fred might even faint.

A hand came from behind Mason and took the revolver out of his holster. Another hand unarmed Felder.

The one with the machine gun said, "Listen close. For the next few hours, you got nothing to do but sit. You just sit, and don't get cute ideas, and you'll be all right. You." He pointed the machine gun at Mason. "What's your name?"

"Officer Mason."

"First name."

"Jim. James."

"All right, Jim. You, what's your name? First name."

"Albert."

"They call you Al, or Bert?"

"Al."

"Okay, Jim, Al, turn around, and do it slow."

They turned around. There were four more of them back there, hooded, in work clothes, one with another Thompson submachine gun, one with another rifle, and two with revolvers. They were just standing there, pointing all that death at Mason and Felder.

The spokesman said, "All right, Jim, Al, you've seen enough. Turn around again."

They turned around. Mason was trying to think, trying to figure out their game. What the hell was all this?

The spokesman was saying, "Who's got the patrol car key?"

Felder said, "Me. I have." Mason was gratified to hear a quaver in Felder's voice; he didn't want either of his brother officers to be less frightened than he was, and he was terrified.

"Bring it over here, Al. Hand it to me."

Felder did as he was told.

"Now go back where you were, Al. The two of you, Al, Jim, get your handcuffs out. Reach them behind you. Don't turn around, Jim, just reach back. Now put your hands together behind you."

Mason put his hands behind his back, and felt the cold metal of the cuffs close around his wrists. He looked at Nieman's face and suddenly realized why Nieman had been so formal when he'd called in; he was trying to warn them.

Mason said, softly, "I'm sorry, Fred, I didn't get it."

"Didn't get what?" It was the one who'd been hidden behind the radio, stepping forward.

Mason closed his mouth. Now he'd done it!

The one with the rifle and the walkie-talkie said, " 'All the world's a stage, and all the men and women merely players.' Fred's seen too many movies. He tried to signal these two by calling them by their last names."

"Son of a bitch!" The one who'd been hidden behind the radio came closer and raised the rifle and slashed at Fred Nieman's head with the butt. Nieman ducked away, raising his arms, and the rifle butt thudded into his shoulder, knocking him down.

The spokesman said sharply. "Cut that out! We need him."

"You hear what he tried to pull?"

"It didn't work. It never does. Fred, how's your shoulder?"

Nieman sat on the floor, holding his shoulder, and didn't speak.

The one who'd hit him said, "You better answer, boy, double quick."

"It's all right."

"Good," said the spokesman. "All right, Al, Jim, come on over this way. Al, lie down between these two desks here. Facedown, that'll be more comfortable, with your hands behind you that way. Jim, you over here between these two desks."

It was tough to get down without his hands to help him. He dropped to his knees and was stuck, until hands came along to lower him more or less gently the rest of the way. He felt his ankles being tied, and then a new voice said, "Open your mouth, Jim."

He opened his mouth. A piece of sponge was stuck into it and then a cloth tied around his head, covering his mouth, to keep the sponge in.

He couldn't see anyone now. All he could see was desk legs and chair legs and the wall. But his ear was pressed against the floor, and he could loudly hear them walking around.

A new voice said, "All right, Fred, get back to the radio. You just sit there, and if a call comes in from anywhere, you handle it like it was a normal night. And don't try anything else cute. I'll know if you do."

It was a familiar voice to Mason, the first familiar voice to come out from one of those black hoods. It was an arrogant voice, and an angry voice, and a familiar voice. Who? Who the hell was it?

All at once he knew, and his terror doubled. He heard the footsteps receding and then the familiar voice saying, "Now we're alone, boys. Just you three and me. And this tommy gun."

Edgars! It was Edgars!

2

Chambers felt all right now, all the nervousness gone, all the jumpiness out of his system. All he'd needed was to get *started*, get *into* this thing. From the second he'd clubbed that smart-ass cop, every bit of jitters just washed right on out of him.

They'd left Edgars in there with the cops, and the other six went outside to stand on the lawn. Parker came over and said, "You got that out of your system now?"

"I guess I do. I feel a lot better."

"Don't do it anymore."

"Not if I don't have to."

"You don't have to club anybody. Watch them if they behave, kill them if they cause trouble. Nothing in between."

"All right by me."

"Good. Everybody set?"

Everybody said they were set. Chambers felt a small irritation, at being chewed out by Parker right there where everybody could hear, but he shrugged it off. Minor irritations couldn't bother him now. He felt good.

Parker had propped the tommy against the outer wall of the police station, and had unlimbered the walkie-talkie. Chambers looked across the street at the fire department building, waiting, and behind him Parker said, "Salsa. You set up?" His voice had an echo, tinny and small, coming out of the walkie-talkie on Grofield's back.

Then it was Salsa's voice, coming over both of them: "Set. I'm in a car on Raymond Avenue, facing out, right side as you are going out of town, one block in from that welcome sign."

"Anybody come in since us?"

"Not in or out."

"All right. Wycza?"

"Here."

"We got police headquarters. Going after the firehouse now. If you see the prowl car, don't worry. I'll be driving it."

Wycza laughed, and said, "Want us to start now?"

"Wait till we've got the firehouse and the telephone company. I'll let you know."

"Right."

Chambers had been fidgeting back and forth, standing in the darkness on the police station lawn. Now he said, "Come on, Parker, let's roll it. We don't got all night."

"Don't be so nervous."

"Then let's just roll, what do you say?"

"All right."

The six of them walked over the lawn and the sidewalk and crossed the street, Chambers in the lead, the rifle held at a loose approximation of port arms. His face was sweating, making the hood stick to his flesh, but he didn't really mind that. Just so they were *moving*.

Too bad Ernie wasn't here.

Four big garage doors, painted red, across the front of the building in a row. To the right of them was the regular entrance, flanked by red lights. Like a cathouse; Chambers grinned under the hood, feeling his skin stretch.

Chambers and Parker were in the lead when they went in. A hall went ahead and then turned right. After the turn, it ran straight and long, but only the nearest fluorescent light was lit, leaving the rest of the hall in darkness. The first door at the right was open, spilling more light into the hall.

Two men in dark-blue uniforms had been sitting on opposite sides of a desk, playing cards. They stared, dropped their cards, and jumped clumsily to their feet. One of them kicked his chair over, getting up.

It was a room very similar to the Command Room in police headquarters, but a little smaller, with fewer desks, fewer pieces of electronic equipment, and less open floor space. Lined around the walls were framed photographs of groups of men standing in front of fire engines, some horse-drawn.

Chambers moved to the left of the door and sensed Parker moving to the right. This was the part he liked, moving fast and moving sure, moving like the pieces of a clock. Let somebody else make the plans; all Chambers wanted was to know his own part in it.

Parker was saying, "You don't have to raise your hands, you aren't armed. You, what's your name?"

"Dee-Deegan."

"First name."

"George."

"And you?"

"Johanson, William Johanson."

"They call you Bill or Will?"

"Uh, Bill."

"All right, Bill, George, just pay attention."

While Parker gave them the spiel, using their first names a lot, telling them how nothing would happen to them if they didn't try nothing stupid, Chambers moved around and pulled a chair out from a desk with his foot and sat down. He kept the rifle level, hoping one of these bastards would make a run for it or something; he'd do just like Parker said, he'd gun him down in a second. But he knew neither of them would try anything; both paunchy geeks in their fifties, scared so bad they had to change their drawers.

Chambers wasn't so sure about Parker. He was supposed to be sharp and cool and efficient and all that, but Chambers wasn't so sure. What was all this crap about the first names? Who cared what kind of first names these stupes had? It was a waste of time.

When Parker was done, Grofield and Phillips came up and hogtied the one named Johanson William Johanson, tying wrists and ankles and gagging him. Then Parker said to the other one, "How many men on tonight?"

"Fuh-four."

"Including you two?"

"Oh no. I'm sorry. S-s-six."

"All right, George, just relax. Nobody's going to hurt you. Where are the other four?"

"Down the hall. They're asleep, mister."

"We'll wake them easy. Which room?"

"Last two on the left."

"Thanks, George." Parker turned his head and spoke to Chambers. "We'll let you know when it's clear."

"Sure thing."

Parker and the others went out to tie and gag the other four sleeping beauties, and Chambers said, sarcastically, "Okay, now, George, just sit right down there. Right there where you were."

George sat down.

"What kind of card game was that, George?"

"Gin."

"Gin. Is that right? You got any of that other kind of gin here, George? You know the kind I mean?"

"No, we don't. I'm sorry, we don't have anything like that."

"That's a real pity, George." Chambers grabbed the bottom of his hood, just under his chin, and flapped it, to get some air inside. "This is a real nice firehouse you got here, George," he said.

"What are you people going to do?"

"Oh, now, don't go asking questions. Remember what happened to that curious cat."

Chambers stretched, and then set the rifle down on the desktop beside him, where it was handy. He said, "You know what you're supposed to do, you get any kind of call, right?"

"Yes. I know."

"Good boy, George. I sure do wish you had some of that other kind of gin."

"I'm sorry. How—how long is this going to be? I mean, before you let us go."

"Curiosity, George."

"But what if there's a fire?"

"Why, we'll just toast marshmallows, George." Chambers laughed, and stuck a hand up under his hood to wipe the sweat from his face.

Parker stuck his head in and said, "Clear. We're moving on now."

"Have a good time, y'all."

"We'll keep you posted. By phone."

Parker went out again.

This was the dull part. From now on, just sitting and waiting, this was going to be the dull part. If Ernie was here, they could Indian wrestle or something. He should of asked to be put on the truck detail, instead of Wycza. Let Wycza sit here all night.

He looked at George, speculatively, trying to find a sign in George's face to indicate he might maybe try something pretty soon, make life interesting somehow. But there was no sense even hoping; George just wasn't the heroic type, that's all there was to it.

He stretched again. He wished he could take the hood off, but he couldn't. He'd taken one fall, and his picture was on file. A dumb fall. Him and Ernie, seventeen years of age for him and nineteen for Ernie, they were just razzing this clown with the tape recorder, down having old rumpots sing folk songs into it, and someway or other it all got out of hand, and when they were done they hadn't just beat the tape recorder in with lumber chunks like they'd intended, they'd beat the clown in, too. Then they had no more sense but to go right straight on home, and get picked up by the sheriff the next morning. Nobody much believed their story about stopping the clown from trying to rape some little girl that run away and likely too mortified to come forward and testify, but they stuck to the story anyway and got smaller sentences than they might of otherwise. Eight years apiece, for manslaughter. Out in less than three years.

There was a time, once, when three years in a state pen couldn't hurt anybody, but that time's long gone. Go look for a job, and the paperwork starts. When was you in the army? Why not? Where were you instead? What were you in the pen for? We'll call you if there's an opening.

Not all jobs were like that. Nobody cares what you did a while back if all they want you for is to operate a shovel or work in a harvest gang. Heavy work for low wages, all you can use.

There's more than one way to make a living. And if you

want more of a living than you can get with a shovel, and if nobody'll give you a sniff at any sort of a job better than that, there's *still* ways to make a living.

Chambers stretched and scratched himself, and watched old George. That damn fool Ernie. Why take off after a sixteen-year-old chippy *anyway*? Who cares how willing she was?

Chambers sighed, and shifted position, and felt the sweat dribbling down. Too bad Ernie wasn't here.

3

Grofield heard background music. Always, everywhere he went. Sometimes lush and full, with a lot of strings. Sometimes rapid-fire, with xylophones and brass, that busy-Manhattan-street-with-yellow-taxicabs music. Sometimes strident, harsh, dramatic. But always music, in the air around his head like a halo.

Right now, next to Parker in the front seat of the patrol car, the music he was hearing was low, slow, like a heavy pulse beat; a bass drum, and a bass fiddle, and maybe a few other instruments, all low-pitched, pounding out a slow relentless beat, gradually building up.

Parker was driving, and wearing a hat he'd taken off one of the cops. The walkie-talkie was on the seat between them, and the tommy between their knees, barrel down against the floor, stock jutting up onto the seat. Grofield's rifle was in his arms, butt in his lap and barrel pointing up past his right ear. His walkie-talkie was on the floor between his legs.

Behind them, in the other car, were Phillips and Littlefield and Kerwin. The two cars drove over Caulkins Street to Raymond Avenue, and turned left. A block and a half up they saw the truck, but nobody in or near it. Grofield heard the music build up in tempo as they went by, rolling slow and silent, Parker's face all jutting angles in the green dashboard lights. Grofield turned his head to look at the truck, anonymous-looking truck, imagining the angle of the follow shot, the camera, having trailed up to now, now speeding, going past on the other side, keeping the truck always centered beyond the patrol car, and intercutting to the faces inside, Parker and himself.

He felt he ought to say something, but nothing came to mind. Nothing that wasn't banal, too damn typical of this scene. None of the really great playwrights had ever written this scene; the fifth-raters who had written it would all, to a man, put in his mouth at this point the line, "Well, this is it, boss."

He remained silent.

Three more blocks and they turned left on Blake Street. The telephone company building was one block over, on the corner. Parker stopped the car, and the background music stopped, too, leaving a dramatic silence. Parker got out of the car, carrying the tommy but leaving the walkie-talkie, and Grofield got out on his side, strapped his walkie-talkie on, and picked up his rifle. The station wagon had stopped behind them, and the other three had got out. They'd all had their hoods off while riding, and now they put them back on.

The telephone company building was three stories high, made of the yellow brick that seemed to be standard around here for nonresidential buildings. The walk up to the door was flanked by flowers. There was a dim light beyond the entrance door, and lights behind four of the windows on the second floor left.

They went in without talking. The walkie-talkie on Grofield's back made a tiny jangling sound as he moved, barely loud enough for even him to hear it. That would be amplified on the soundtrack, serve instead of background music. He tried to walk so as to give the jangling a proper slow rhythm.

Inside, a globe hanging from the ceiling was lit, showing a hall, and a wide flight of metal stairs leading up. They went up, sliding their feet onto each step with small shushing sounds, to avoid any clatter, and at the top they saw a door with light behind the frosted glass.

They pushed open the door and went in, Parker first, Grofield after him, and the others behind. Parker said, "Stop, ladies. If anybody screams, I shoot."

Three women. One at a desk, writing with a ballpoint pen. The other two on chairs before a long switchboard filling the right-hand wall, looking like a flat back computer. All three stared. Two opened their mouths, but none of them screamed.

Parker said, "All stand up. Move to the center of the room."

The woman at the desk found part of her voice and said, "What are you men doing here?"

"Do as the gentleman tells you, dear," said Grofield. "Don't interfere with the schedule."

He watched the three women move uncertainly to the center of the room. The two operators looked terrified, period. The woman who'd been at the desk looked both terrified and indignant. But there wouldn't be any screaming, and there wouldn't be any running or anything like that. They'd behave.

Parker lowered the tommy and pointed at the woman from the desk. "What's your name?"

"Mrs. Sawyer."

"What's your first name, Mrs. Sawyer?"

"Edith."

"Introduce me to the other ladies, Edith."

"I don't know what you have in—"

"Just tell me their names, Edith."

One of the operators blurted, "I'm Linda Peters."

"Thank you, Linda. What's your friend's name?"

The friend spoke for herself. "Mary Deegan."

"Mary Deegan. Tell me, Mary, you related to George Deegan, over at the firehouse?"

"He's my uncle."

"Well, he's in good hands, Mary. Just like you."

Grofield liked to watch Parker work. See him before a job, or after, you'd think he was just a silent heavy, quick-tempered and mean, about as subtle as a gorilla. But on a job, dealing with any people that might be in the way, he was all psychology.

Terrify them first. Terrify them in such a way that they'll freeze. Not so they'll make noise, or run, or jump you, or anything like that, just so they'll freeze. Then talk to them, calm and gentle. Get their first names, and use the first names. When a man uses your first name, calmly and without sarcasm, he's accepting your individuality, your worthiness to live. The use of your first name implies that this man really doesn't want to harm you.

The fright to freeze them, and then the reassurance to keep them frozen. And it worked almost every time.

Parker was explaining it to them now, telling them all they had to know. He was telling them he was sorry two of them would have to be tied and gagged, but it wouldn't be for long. They were watching him, the three of them, hanging on his words.

That was another part of the psychology. Bunch them together right away, in a little group. It reassures them, to be in a group, and it cuts down the possibility of individual initiative. Each member of the group waits for some other member of the group to lead the way.

Parker even arranged the tying and gagging differently. Phillips and Littlefield brought over two of the chairs, took the casters off them so they wouldn't roll, and had Mrs. Edith Sawyer and Linda Peters sit down in them. Their ankles were tied to the center chair leg, their wrists were tied behind their backs, and the sponge-and-cloth gags were applied. Then Parker and the others left, and Grofield was on his own.

The operator still loose was Mary Deegan. Grofield said to her, "Mary, do you suppose there's a telephone book around here anywhere?"

"Well, yes. Of course." Her fright was fading, and she was now becoming bewildered.

"Good. Mary, I want you to get that book, and sit down at Edith's desk there, and copy down some phone numbers for me. Will you do that like a good girl?"

"The book's in the desk drawer."

"Well, then, get it."

She went over and sat behind the desk, and looked at him doubtfully. "It's all right for me to open the drawer?"

"Mary, you don't have a gun in that drawer. And if you do, you have more sense than to show it to me. Go ahead and open the drawer."

She opened the drawer, and put the phone book on the desk.

"Good girl. Now, give me the phone number for police headquarters. Got it? Now the firehouse."

She looked up. "Do you really have my uncle prisoner, too?"

"Tut, tut! Prisoner me no prisoner, nor uncle me no uncle." Though she couldn't see it under the hood, he smiled, then said, "A paraphrase of Shakespeare. Your uncle is in good hands. Write down the number, and maybe later you can talk to him."

She wrote down the number.

"Let's see. One more. The night phone at the refinery."

She wrote that one, too.

"Good girl. Just leave the paper there, and rise and go to yon computer, if you would. Resume your seat there." He sat down at the desk, put the rifle down on its top, and pointed to the phone in front of him. "Can I work this? Or do you have to do something there?"

"You can work it."

"Fine." He picked up the receiver, and dialed police headquarters.

It was answered after one ring: "Police headquarters, Officer Nieman." The officer's voice sounded a little thin and strained.

"Hello, Fred, let me talk to E. The man with the machine gun." He felt the women's eyes on his face as he said the last words, and even though he wore a hood he forced himself not to smile.

Edgars came on the line, sounding wary. "Yeah?"

"G here at the phone company. Everything's fine. You can reach me at 7-3060. Got that?"

"Got it. Everything's under control here, too. You're the first call."

"May I be the only."

"Right."

Grofield broke the connection and called the firehouse. The shaky voice this time said only, "Hello?"

"Hello, George. I want to talk to C."

"Who?"

"The man with the rifle."

"Oh. Oh!"

Chambers came on, saying, "How's it going, man?"

"Fine. Everything under control. Let me give you the number here, in case you have to reach me."

"Hold on. George, give me a pencil. And a sheet of paper. Okay, go ahead."

Grofield gave him the number, and then hung up and got to his feet. He took the walkie-talkie off, set it on the desk next to the rifle, and hunched his shoulders to get the stiffness out of them. He looked over at Mary Deegan and said, "Mary, you got direct distance dialing here?"

"Not yet."

"If anybody wants to call out of town, they've got to go through you, right?"

"Yes."

"Good." He picked up the rifle and walked across the room to her. "If anybody calls you, I want to listen in. How do we work that?"

"You could sit there, I guess. Put that headset on, and plug that jack in there."

"Fine. Now we're set, aren't we?"

"I suppose so."

Grofield leaned back in the chair, feeling the unfamiliar closeness of the headset against his ears. The music had a high richness to it now, and he was bringing it back from over Germany, the copilot dead in the seat beside him. They'd said daylight low-level precision bombing was impossible, but he'd helped to prove them wrong. Radio silence, radio silence. The earphones were silent on his head.

Six years, eleven jobs. Every one of them had had the moments of high drama, complete with music and camera angles and dramatic lighting effects but they'd all had stretches like this, too, of waiting, silence, and boredom.

Twenty thousand. Maybe more. Too late to get into summer stock now, but there was always winter stock in Florida or Texas or somewhere. This time, why not spend the money the smart way? Produce. Get into the money end of the damn racket for once.

But you couldn't produce stock and act in it both. He'd already tried it, in Maine, three summers ago. But he liked to act and he hated paperwork, and the summer had been a disaster. So he'd do the same as always, act for peanuts in winter stock, throw away the dough on a convertible and a good apartment and good times, and by the end of the season he'd be broke again, looking around for another job. Number twelve.

All except number one had been fine. Competent professional jobs, because he was working with the right people. The first one had been a mess. Begun as a gag, actually gone through with only because nobody wanted to be the first to quit, and successful by pure luck.

In Pennsylvania it was. A repertory company, twelve of them on a shares basis, and the company not even earning enough to maintain itself. Four of the guys had started talking about stealing, as a gag: "If business keeps up this lousy, we'll have to knock over a gas station or two." Then the gag got specific; a supermarket in a suburban area forty miles away.

When it stopped being a gag and started being reality Grofield couldn't say for sure. But it became reality, as they worked out plan after plan for weeks, and then they went ahead and did it, wearing masks, carrying prop guns loaded with blanks, in an old beat-up Chevrolet with mud smeared on the license plates. They got forty-three hundred dollars, and they never were caught.

That was number one, and afterward Grofield swore it would never happen again; you couldn't bank on dumb luck forever. But he was still in general contact with a guy he'd known in the army, and one time he mentioned the super-market score to him—the only one he'd told about it, up till then—and the guy laughed and offered him a spot driving in a jewelry store heist. It was just driving the car, and he was broke again, summer stock being over and nothing having turned up in the city. So he did it.

And he was still doing it. He was probably the only actor in the United States who could really afford to work at Equity minimum.

Over on the desk, the walkie-talkie spoke, in a tin imitation of Parker's voice, saying, "Radio station taken care of. Nobody was there."

Wycza's voice said, "Shall we start?"

"Wait till we get the west gate."

"It's almost twelve-thirty."

"I know."

Mary Deegan said, suddenly, "You're going to steal the payroll, aren't you?"

"Ask me no questions, I'll tell you no lies. I tell you what, let's play Twenty Questions. You know how to play Twenty Questions?"

"Wha-what?"

"Twenty Questions. Do you know how to play it?"

She nodded, doubtfully.

"Good." He looked around, saw the walkie-talkie. "I'm thinking of something mineral."

All at once she started to cry. She ducked her head and whispered, "I'm, I'm sorry. It's my nerves."

"That's all right, Mary. It's just stage fright, don't worry about it."

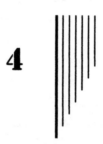

4

Kerwin didn't take any part in wrecking the radio station
equipment. For himself, he didn't even think it was necessary,
but Parker and the others did, so let them do it.

He stood in the doorway, watching the street. The prowl
car was parked there, at the curb, with the station wagon behind it. There was absolute silence from the street, but from
inside there were the crashes of metallic breakage.

Kerwin liked metal. He liked machinery, liked to watch it
work, liked to fiddle with it and learn about it and understand it. At home, he was a ham radio operator, and a do-it-
yourselfer. He owned two prewar cars, and they both ran like
watches. In one corner of his basement there was a model
train layout, full of drawbridges and complex signal systems;
he ran the model railroad with his neighbor, and two pipes
under the driveway between their houses carried track which
linked their systems.

He liked machinery and he hated to see it destroyed. When it came to safes, he liked to use drill and screwdriver and wrench and his own hands; men who relied on nitro were just bums and amateurs, not professional safe men at all. And when it came to the kind of wreckage Parker and Littlefield and Phillips were doing in the radio station now, Kerwin wanted no part of it. He didn't approve.

The sounds stopped. A few seconds later, they came out, all wearing their hoods, and Parker said, "Clear?"

Kerwin nodded. "Clear."

They went out and got into the two cars, Parker and Phillips in the prowl car, Kerwin and Littlefield in the wagon. They drove back up Whittier to Raymond, turned left, and drove down to the end, to the west gate of the plant.

This part had no effect on Kerwin at all. People were just fuses; they had to be deactivated before you could get to work. He and Littlefield waited while the patrol car nosed forward to the gate, and the guard came out of his booth, waving in a friendly way. Then the guard stopped, and raised his hands, and Kerwin saw Phillips get out of the car, walk around it, disarm the guard, and walk him back into his shack.

Littlefield cleared his throat and said, "Think they need us?"

"If they do, they'll motion to us."

"I guess so."

Parker had got out of the car now, too, and had gone into the shack. After a couple of minutes, Phillips came out wearing the guard's uniform. He attached a metal sign to the already closed gate, and got into the car just as Parker also came out of the shack.

Littlefield cleared his throat again. "It's certainly running smooth," he said.

Kerwin glanced at him and saw how tightly he was holding the steering wheel. "Nothing to be nervous about," he said.

"That's right." Littlefield coughed, and cleared his throat.

The prowl car had backed away from the gate, and swung to the right. Littlefield put the wagon in gear, and followed the prowl car down Copper Street toward the other gate. Closed luncheonettes and bars and barber shops and tailors were on their right, and the fence on their left. Beyond the fence were the dark bulks of the plant buildings, and beyond them, in total darkness, the sheer wall of the canyon.

Again, the station wagon hung back while the prowl car drove up to the gate. The same actions were repeated, and then Parker waved to them to come forward. Phillips had opened the gate, and was standing there looking natural and easy in the guard uniform. He gave them a mock salute as the wagon passed him, following Parker along the blacktop company street between the buildings.

By the time Littlefield stopped in front of the main building, Kerwin had his bag of tools ready in his lap. They got out of the car, joined Parker, and the three of them went into the building.

As far as Kerwin was concerned, defusing people was Parker's job. Kerwin's job was simply to stand there and add numerical strength. He entered the office with Parker and Littlefield, and belatedly drew the revolver from his shoulder holster. Guns were about the only machines he wasn't interested in; he held this one absentmindedly, waiting without listening while Parker talked to the frightened man awhile, and then Parker and Littlefield tied and gagged him. Once they were done, he put the revolver away again—the safety hadn't been off yet tonight—and said, "Where is it?"

"Through here."

Littlefield was sitting at the desk now, clearing his throat and watching the telephone. Kerwin followed Parker through a doorway, across an office, down a hall, and through another office. He waited while Parker forced a locked door, then went into the room and looked at the safe.

It was dark green, with yellow designs. Approximate exterior dimensions, four feet high, two and a half feet wide, three feet deep. Simple combination lock. Parker had turned on the office lights, because the windows here faced the rear of the building. Kerwin walked over and set his bag on a desk and patted the top of the safe.

Parker said, "You all set?"

"Mmm? Yes, of course."

5

Paulus sat on the floor in the back of the truck, and fidgeted. It was pitch black in the truck, nothing to see, nothing to do. Paulus liked to be able to observe what was going on, to see symmetry in the motion around him, and to see whether or not things were going right. Sitting here in the truck, in darkness, while actions important to him were going on outside, was torture.

From time to time, Wycza's walkie-talkie spoke out in Parker's voice, saying where they were, what they'd done. That they'd ruined the equipment in the radio station. A little later, that they'd captured the guard on the west gate. Just the bare facts, unadorned.

It wasn't enough. Paulus wanted to be able to *see*. He wanted to look at the radio station equipment and *know* it was no longer workable. He wanted to see the guard, find out his name, watch his reactions, gauge the possible danger he might be in during the course of the night. He wanted to know precisely the situation at the telephone company, the firehouse, the police station. He wanted to see exactly where Salsa was stationed near the town line. He wanted to have a clipboard, and a list, and a pencil with which to check off completed items satisfactorily handled. He wanted to see symmetry and balance and precision.

A match flared; Wycza lighting a stub of cigar. In the small light, Paulus again saw the plank floor and metal side of the truck, saw Wycza and Wiss and Elkins sitting, like himself, on the floor, saw his own sturdy suitcase full of tools and the weatherbeaten black bag—like a doctor's bag—in which Wiss kept his equipment. He looked at his watch, but he wasn't fast enough; Wycza blew out the match.

He shook his head in annoyance. It was important to know the time, know whether or not they were keeping to the schedule. He reached for his own matches.

But a clinging self-consciousness wouldn't let him light a match just to see his watch; he didn't want the others to know he felt that strongly about knowing the time. So he got out his cigarettes, too, though he didn't particularly want a cigarette. He struck the match, lit the cigarette, and kept the match aflame till he'd read his watch.

Twelve thirty-five.

Not too bad. He'd be in at the bank vault well before one. He shook the match out, and sat holding the cigarette, not smoking it.

The walkie-talkie spoke again: "Got the east gate. Going into the main office now. You can get started, W."

They had to use the initials because of Grofield. He was at the telephone company, with one of the walkie-talkies, and the women there could hear everything it said. It was Paulus who'd suggested the initials.

Wycza was saying, "Okay. You gonna patrol now?"

"After we get the main office."

"Check."

Paulus clambered to his feet, felt around in the dark, and picked up his suitcase. He moved toward the rear of the truck, and before he got there Elkins pushed the door open and jumped down to the street. Elkins reached up and took the black bag from Wiss, and Wiss clambered down more carefully. Paulus waited for Wycza, and as Wycza passed said, "You go first, I'll hand you my suitcase."

"Sure."

Being the last out, Paulus was careful to close the truck doors again. He took the suitcase back from Wycza and stepped up on the sidewalk. Wiss and Elkins had already started across the street.

Directly ahead of Paulus was the Merchants' Bank building, with the offices of Nationwide Finance & Loan Corporation on the second floor. The building was modernistic, made mostly of glass and chrome. Even the doors were mainly glass.

Paulus set his suitcase down near the doors and waited for Wycza to let him in. Wycza got his revolver from its shoulder holster, and used the butt to break the door glass. There were quieter, more scientific ways to do it, but they weren't worried about noise here, and the scientific ways were all slower. Wycza reached through, unlocked the doors from the inside, and pushed them open.

Paulus followed him inside. Wycza had put his revolver away now and taken out a flashlight. The narrow beam showed wood-paneled counters with marble tops, and cream composition flooring, and a free-form copper bas-relief sprawled out on one wall. The vault door was in plain sight on the rear wall, huge and round and complex, looking like an escape hatch on a spaceship or the entrance to a torpedo tube in a submarine.

After the front door, there were no more obstacles to the vault, no doors to unlock or gates to jimmy. They lifted a flap at the end of the counter, walked through the loan department, took a left around a railing, and there was the vault door in front of them. Desks and railings and countertops hid them almost completely from the street.

While Wycza held the flashlight, Paulus studied the vault door. He nodded in recognition of the type, walked back and forth to consider it from various angles, and rubbed the knuckles of his hands together as he thought it out. Drill four holes, load, blast. He pursed his lips, and nodded. Now he was absorbed, completely absorbed.

Wycza said, "Any problems?"

"I don't think so. Shine the light here a minute."

He knelt and opened the suitcase, got the drill, selected a

bit, changed his mind and selected another. He looked around and said, "Find me an outlet."

"Over here."

"Am I going to need the extension?"

"No," Wycza laughed. "Handy, huh? The architect had you in mind."

"Good of him." Paulus carried the drill over to the vault, went down on one knee. "Hold the light steady, now."

The drill began to whine.

6

He'd missed the curfew.

His name was Eddie Wheeler, he was nineteen years old, he worked at Brooks' Pharmacy, and he was now in the Campbell house, having been engaged in premarital intercourse with Betty Campbell, whose parents were visiting relatives all this week in Bismarck.

He'd fallen asleep, entwined in Betty's arms.

"It's one o'clock," he whispered. There wasn't any need to whisper—he and Betty were the only ones in the house—but he whispered anyway. For the same lack of reason, they hadn't turned on any lights, but depended on the illumination coming faintly through the window from a streetlight outside.

"What are you going to do?" Betty was half sitting, half lying on the bed, holding a sheet up to her throat.

Eddie felt around on the floor for his other shoe. "What can I do? I've got to get home."

"Stay here tonight."

"And what do I tell my folks? Where do I say I spent all night?"

"But what if the police catch you?"

"What can they do to me?" He found the other shoe, put it on, tied the laces. "They'll just give me a warning, that's all."

"It's my fault, Eddie, I shouldn't have gone to sleep."

"We *both* went to sleep." He got to his feet. "I'll call you tomorrow."

"Wait, I'll walk you downstairs."

"No, stay there, go back to sleep."

"I've got to lock the door anyway."

He was concentrating so hard on getting away, slipping across town to his own house without being caught by the police, that he barely paid attention to her when she got out of bed, slim and pale and naked as a nymph, and quickly shrugged into a bathrobe. Almost six months they'd been sleeping together now, and she still got into a robe anytime she got out of bed, still covered herself with a sheet before and after, still made him turn his back while she undressed and got into bed. It was silly, but there it was. And it was a small price to pay.

Six months, and this was the first time anything had distracted him from staring at any rare glimpse of her she offered. The goddam curfew.

They went down the carpeted stairs together, she barefoot, and over to the front door. His heart was pounding, he felt like a desperado. He opened the door a little and peeked out, and saw no cars moving, no people at all. "I'll call you tomorrow," he whispered.

"Kiss me good night, Eddie."

"Oh. I forgot."

She was soft and warm from bed, and he forgot his nervousness for a few seconds, caught up in the sense of her. But the breeze from the slightly open door was cool on the back of his neck, reminding him, and he was the first to break the kiss. He told her again he'd call her tomorrow. Her robe had parted, and her breasts were pale and full and soft, but he turned away and sidled out onto the porch. They whispered good night to each other, and she closed the door. He heard the snick of the lock.

Nothing moving. Orange Street was dark and silent. A block and a half away, Raymond Avenue was a bit brighter, but just as silent. It was after one o'clock in the morning.

Which would they patrol most, Raymond Avenue or the side streets? Raymond Avenue was so brightly lit, a curfewbreaker might tend to keep away from it; wouldn't the police think of that? They'd patrol the side streets most, wouldn't they? And just cross Raymond Avenue from time to time, going from one side of town to the other?

All right. So he'd go straight to Raymond Avenue, and down Raymond to Blake Street, and then over Blake Street the two blocks to his house. On Orange and Blake, he could duck into a driveway if he saw headlights. On Raymond, he could hide in a store doorway.

Reluctantly, he left the protection of the porch, went down to the sidewalk, and turned right. He walked along quickly, his shoulders hunched, his hands in his pants pockets. He kept looking back over his shoulder, but he didn't see any headlights.

Raymond Avenue. He turned left. He went half a block, and out of the corner of his eye he saw something wrong.

Broken glass.

The bank door was broken.

He stopped in his tracks, forgetting everything else, and stared at the broken glass of the bank door. Parked here was a big brown tractor trailer, but nobody in or near it. But in the bank . . .

He went over to the glass front and peered in. There was a light back there, he could just barely make it out. And a man standing there.

Bank robbers!

He took three quick steps, beyond the bank's glass front. Had they seen him? He didn't think so. No, they would have come after him. Bank robbers, and that must be their truck.

What in hell was he going to do? He stared around wildly, and two blocks farther down, at the corner of Whittier Street, he could see the telephone booth. There was a phone booth right on the corner there, he'd used it himself a few times. He could go there and phone police headquarters.

Where was the police car? A minute ago he'd been grateful for its absence, but now he felt indignant that it wasn't here. That was the police for you, never around when you wanted them. If there weren't any bank robbers, the police car would be right here this second, the cops giving him a bad time for being out after curfew.

Did he dare phone in? He was still breaking the law himself.

Don't be silly. Giving the warning about a bank robbery would make up for being out late. They wouldn't even mention it.

He started off again, this time going at a trot, hurrying down the two blocks to Whittier Street, looking down the cross streets in hopes of seeing the headlights of the police car, but seeing nothing. At the phone booth, he paused to catch his breath and to find a dime, and then he stepped into the booth and closed the door. It was a glass-and-metal booth, mostly windows, and when he closed the door the light came on. Startled, he snapped the door open again, and the light went off. That was all he needed, the light on, so the robbers could see him making the call.

He did it the simplest way. Dropped the dime in, dialed Operator, and when the girl came on said, "Police headquarters, please. This is an emergency."

"Yes, sir."

It seemed like a pretty long pause, but finally he heard a ringing sound, and then a male voice said, "Police headquarters, Officer Nieman."

"I . . ." He didn't know how to phrase it. He cleared his throat, and blurted it out: "There's a bank robbery going on! The Merchants' Bank."

"What? Who are you?"

"Eddie Wheeler. They broke the door, and they're back by the vault."

"What are you doing out at this time of night?"

"For Pete's sake, will you listen to me? There's a—"

It was like a crack of thunder, the sudden sound, not too far away. Eddie looked up, startled, knowing they'd blown open the vault door. "They just blew up the vault!"

A different voice answered him. "Where are you?"

"I'm in the phone booth at Raymond and Whittier."

"Stay there, the prowl car will be right there."

"All right."

The connection was broken.

Even with the light off, Eddie felt exposed, in the glass phone booth. He stepped out, and went over to lean against the side of the nearest building, Komray's Department Store. He stared down toward the bank, waiting and watching, wondering what was keeping the police.

The prowl car, when it arrived, came without siren or flashing red light. It seemed to roll along leisurely, and then it stopped at the curb by the phone booth. Eddie stepped toward it, away from the wall, and saw the driver getting out. "They're down at the Merch—"

The driver was wearing a hood.

Eddie just stared at him. The driver came around the front of the car, and he was holding a pistol aimed right at Eddie's stomach. He said, "You ought to know better than to be out after curfew, Eddie."

"You're one of them!"

"Walk down Whittier, Eddie. Ahead of me. Do like you're told and you won't get hurt."

Eddie turned, and started walking. He didn't believe it, didn't believe that he wouldn't get hurt. He was going to be murdered, he knew it.

He thought of Betty's breasts, gleaming behind the robe. He thought of her asking him to stay the night. He thought of sex with her, thought of the glimpses of her body.

Why didn't I stay?

"Turn right, Eddie."

It was the loading dock behind the department store. God, it was dark back there! Eddie hesitated, and the hooded man said, "I don't want to kill you, Eddie. I got nothing against you. I'm going to tie you and gag you, and early in the morning somebody'll find you here, safe and sound. But if you try anything cute, I'll have to cut you down."

Eddie swallowed, painfully.

"Why you out after curfew anyway, Eddie?"

"I wish I knew."

He walked into the darkness.

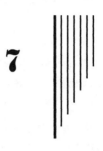

7

One A.M.

Most of Copper Canyon was asleep. Three policemen, six firemen, three telephone company employees, three plant employees, and a boy named Eddie Wheeler were all awake. Most of these were tied and gagged; none of them was sure he'd live till morning. Aside from these sixteen, there were about twenty other citizens awake in Copper Canyon; insomniacs reading, couples making love, two young mothers warming baby bottles.

The Merchants' Bank and City Trust had both been blown open. Wycza was carrying trays of money from Merchants' to the truck, Elkins was carrying trays of money from City to the truck. Paulus was working on the Nationwide Finance & Loan Corporation safe, and Wiss was working on the Raymond Jewelers safe. At the plant, Kerwin hadn't yet opened the safe containing the payroll; he worked slowly, because he enjoyed his work.

Parker was in the prowl car, driving aimlessly this way and that, the walkie-talkie on the seat beside him. At the firehouse, Chambers had commandeered the playing cards and was dealing out hand after hand of solitaire, waiting for George to make a run for the door. At the telephone company, Grofield was playing charades with George's niece Mary; she was laughing. At police headquarters, in the Command Room, Edgars sat inside his hood and brooded on his own plans.

Pop Phillips was half asleep, sitting on a tilted-back chair in the guard shack by the east gate. In the main plant building, Littlefield sat in a coil of tension, waiting for the phone to ring and wondering what he would do if it did. At the other end of town, Salsa sat with stolid patience in a brand-new Oldsmobile, watching the empty street. There was a car a little ways ahead, parked at the curb, and a streetlight shone on its license plate, a dull tan with the number in dark brown. Below the number was the legend PEACE GARDEN STATE; Salsa wondered idly what that meant.

TWO A.M.

Eddie Wheeler was asleep, his face against cold asphalt. In the morning he would have the beginnings of a bad head cold, but he'd be alive. Officer Mason, three firemen, and Mrs. Sawyer at the phone company were all also asleep, leaving ten of the prisoners still awake.

Kerwin had finished the plant safe, finally, and loaded the payroll into the station wagon. He had driven down Raymond Avenue to the truck, transferred the payroll—in white canvas bank bags—to the truck, and carried his bag of tools to Credit Jewelers, where he was now once again opening a safe. Paulus was walking through Komray's Department Store with a flashlight, looking for the office. Wiss had just left the five-and-dime and was entering the shoe store next door. Wycza and Elkins were loading the truck.

Pop Phillips was asleep. Littlefield was chain-smoking. Salsa was standing beside the Oldsmobile, stretching his legs. Chambers was cheating at solitaire. Parker was driving around in the patrol car. Edgars was moodily studying the submachine gun, waiting for the time to be right. Grofield knew Mary Deegan wanted him to kiss her, but he couldn't figure out how to do it without removing the hood.

Three A.M.

Five prisoners remained awake: Officer Nieman, George Deegan and his niece, one other fireman, and the guard from the west gate. All other citizens were asleep, except one insomniac who had chapters to go in the mystery he was reading.

Wiss and Paulus and Kerwin were opening safes; Wycza and Elkins were emptying them. Salsa was back in the Oldsmobile, thinking of women. Edgars was growing impatient. Grofield's hood was off; so were Mary Deegan's panties.

Three forty-five A.M.

Wycza opened a cab door of the truck, stepped up, sat down to rest a minute, and switched on his walkie-talkie. "This is W," he said. "You there, P?" He felt stupid, using initials; you might know Paulus would dream up something like that.

Parker answered: "What's up?"

"Everything's open. We'll be done quicker than we thought. All five of us are loading now."

"How much longer?"

"Half an hour, maybe less."

"S, you hear that?"

Salsa picked up the walkie-talkie. "I hear it. That's very good." He put the walkie-talkie down on the seat again and lit a new cigarette.

Parker said, "G, you there?"

Grofield had been trying to explain to Mary Deegan why he couldn't take her along, and she'd begun to get mad, had just pointed out that she could identify him now. He was grateful for the interruption. He went over and picked up the walkie-talkie and said, "Right here."

"Spread the word. We'll be ready to clear out in half an hour."

"Right."

Grofield went over to the desk and picked up the phone. Mary followed him, saying, "I don't see why you can't take me."

"In a minute, all right? Just one minute." He dialed police

headquarters, went through Officer Nieman, got Edgars, told him, "We'll be moving out in half an hour."

"So soon? Thanks." Edgars hung up, picked up the machine gun, and sprayed bullets into Officers Nieman and Mason and Felder. He went down the well-remembered hall to the armory, shot the lock off, went in and opened the metal box in the corner. World War II souvenirs, impounded by the police, including three live hand grenades. He took them, left the building, and went across the street to the firehouse.

Grofield's second call was to Littlefield, who jumped when the phone rang as though he'd been hit by a live wire. He fumbled the receiver, dropped it, picked it up again, and tried to clear his throat while he was saying hello. Grofield told him about the speed-up, and Littlefield nearly fainted from relief. But after that, he wasn't tense anymore; if the phone rang again, no matter who it was calling, he wouldn't be nervous or frightened at all.

Grofield called the firehouse, got Chambers, and said, "It's running faster that we thought. We'll be going in about half an hour."

"Boy, you'll never know how— Hey!"

"What?"

It sounded like a machine gun, roaring away there at the other end. Then the line went dead.

Forgetting himself, Grofield shouted, "Chambers! Chambers!" But the line was dead.

Mary was staring at him wide-eyed. "What is it? What's

the matter?" The other two women were stirring, disturbed out of sleep.

Grofield had the walkie-talkie now, was saying, "P. Listen, something's gone wrong."

"What?"

"The firehouse. I don't know what it is. Sounded like machine gun fire, and then we were cut off."

Parker cursed, and said, "W, you hear that?"

"I hear it."

"Take the wagon. I'll meet you at the firehouse."

The first explosion woke Pop Phillips. He jumped up, startled, looking around, not knowing what had knocked him out of sleep.

Parker heard the explosion, cursed again, and gunned the prowl car forward.

Citizens heard the explosion, and some of them started phoning police headquarters to find out what it was, but nobody answered at police headquarters. Some of them dialed Operator, but no operator answered either; Mary Deegan was trying to get Grofield's attention, and failing.

The firehouse was on fire, half the front wall had been blown away, and, inside, flames leaped around the fire engines as the gasoline in their tanks burned. Parker got out of the prowl car, looking around, and didn't see Chambers or anyone else. The station wagon raced up, squealed to a stop, and Wycza jumped out, saying, "What the hell happened?"

"I don't know. Come on."

They went across the street to the police station. Edgars was nearest; he ought to know what had happened.

Edgars wasn't in the Command Room. Phones were ringing, but Officer Nieman lay bleeding in the middle of the floor, nearly shot in two.

"Edgars," said Wycza.

Parker grimaced. "I knew there was something wrong with that bastard, I knew it."

Wycza said, "One of them groaned." He went over, knelt, said, "This one's alive."

It was Officer Mason. He whispered, "Edgars. Edgars."

"Yeah," said Wycza. "We know."

Parker came over. "Did he say Edgars? Does he know Edgars?"

Officer Mason whispered again, and Wycza leaned close to hear him. Parker watched impatiently, and said, "What did he say?"

Wycza looked up. "Chief of police. Edgars used to be chief of police here."

The second explosion was a lot bigger than the first.

8

He hadn't wanted to kill Chambers, but Chambers had tried to get in his way. He didn't know what the others would think of that; they might be sore at him, but it didn't matter. he wasn't interfering with them, and they shouldn't interfere with him.

He came up to the east gate, and Pop Phillips came out of the shack, saying, "What the hell was that explosion?"

"A vault, I guess. There's something I've got to do in here."

"A vault?" Phillips frowned. "They don't need *that* much nitro," he said.

Edgars went on by him, and walked along the company road. He knew which building contained the furnaces and fuel; he went straight to it, and there he used the second of his grenades. He threw it, then flattened himself behind a wall, but the explosion knocked him off his feet anyway.

He picked himself up, found the machine gun, and started

running. He ran back to the gate, and Phillips shouted, "What's going on?"

"Just stay there! Stick to your position!"

Edgars ran down Copper Street toward Raymond Avenue. Off to his right, part of the plant had started to burn; orange flames were shooting up, dirtying the night sky.

"Good-bye, Copper Canyon. I'll burn you to the ground."

He turned at Hector Avenue. Hector was four blocks east of, and parallel with, Raymond Avenue. The railroad station was on Hector Avenue, two blocks away.

They'd never proved anything on him, the bastards. People had sat there in front of that grand jury and spouted all their stories about him, but they'd never been able to prove a thing. Brutality? A kickback from Regal Ford on the purchase of the new patrol car? Kickbacks from the suppliers of radio equipment, weapons and ammunition, uniforms, all the rest of it? You needed witnesses, you needed *proof*. Well they couldn't get proof. He wasn't dumb enough to be caught by these hicks, not in a million years.

They couldn't return a single indictment, not a one. On over fifty charges of one kind and another, they hadn't been able to dredge up enough proof to hit him with even one little indictment. He laughed at them. He sat there as safe as houses, and laughed at them.

So they threw him out. The call to the mayor's office, and the whole crowd there; Thorndike, the mayor, and Ableman, the general manager of the plant, and all the rest of them. Notoriety, they said. Bad press. The lost confidence of the voters. They wanted his resignation.

"But the grand jury cleared me!"

Ableman was the one who answered him: "No, they didn't. They couldn't pin anything on you, but they didn't clear you."

"You don't get any resignation from me."

Thorndike: "It'll look worse for you if I have to dismiss you."

"You do, and you'll regret it."

But he did. And he was going to regret it.

Just ahead was the railroad station. And just beyond it was Ekonomee Gas.

Ekonomee Gas was a filling station, an independent not connected with any of the major gasoline companies. Ekonomee, like many similar independents, had no underground storage tanks. The station was built next to the railroad line, and a short spur track ran across the rear of the station property. Ekonomee bought gasoline in tank car lots, and piped the gas straight from the tank car into the pumps. There were always three or four tank cars full of gasoline on the spur behind Ekonomee Gas.

That was the place for the last grenade. That one ought to start a lovely fire. Two fires then, one at the plant and one at Ekonomee. Maybe three, if the firehouse had caught. In any case, they'd have plenty of time to spread. There was no longer any fire-fighting equipment in town. The radio station was disabled, the transmitting equipment at police headquarters had been riddled with machine-gun bullets, and once he'd blown up Ekonomee he'd go over to the telephone company and put *that* out of commission.

No fire-fighting equipment in town, and no way to call to Madison or anywhere else to get some help. It would be hours before they could get organized to fight the fire, hours. With luck, the whole goddam town would burn down.

And Parker and the others would have to help. All this racket would attract the attention of the state police, at the barracks down 22A. Parker and the others would have to put that barracks out of commission; they'd have no choice.

"I *told* you you'd regret it, Thorndike!"

He ran past the railroad station, over the blacktop driveway of Ekonomee and around the corner of the building. Three tank cars there. The spreading fire back at the plant glinted in smudged reflection on their sides.

Edgars paused at the corner of the building. He had the last grenade in his hands, and heard someone shout his name. He turned and saw two of the others running toward him, the prowl car standing behind them. "Keep away!" he shouted. "Keep away!"

"Stop!"

He pulled the pin. He whirled, and threw the grenade at the tank cars.

9

The blast knocked Wycza off his feet. He went sprawling, his revolver flying out of his hand. He rolled and started to his feet, and a second blast knocked him down again. He was a wrestler sometimes and his body reacted instinctively to a lack of balance, adjusting itself, shifting, rolling, avoiding falls that could hurt.

He made it to his feet this time, and saw Parker braced against one of the pumps. The gas-station building had fallen forward, and leaping flames behind it lit the whole area. He looked around but couldn't see Edgars.

He shouted the name, and Parker shook his head, pointing at the rubble. "Under there."

"We've got to get out of here, Parker."

"I know."

They ran back to the car, and Parker got his walkie-talkie. "G! Get hold of Littlefield, fast. Tell him to get down to the east gate, we'll pick him up there. Then you get over to Raymond, on the double."

Wycza, getting into the prowl car on the passenger side, heard Grofield's voice saying, "What the hell's going on?"

"Later. Get moving. S, watch that road, the troopers may come in. If they do, don't stop them, just warn us."

Salsa's voice said, "Will do."

"I never did like that trooper barracks," said Wycza. "I never did."

Parker had started the prowl car. He spun out away from the station, headed toward Raymond Avenue.

People were coming out on the sidewalks. Some of them, recognizing the patrol car, waved their arms, wanting the police to stop and answer questions. Wycza looked at them and muttered, "It's sour, Parker. It's gone sour."

"I know. You drive the truck, I'll take the wagon. Get your people in it and get going. Pick up Salsa and Grofield. I'll get Littlefield and Phillips."

"Right."

Raymond Avenue. Parker turned the wheel hard right, and braked next to the truck. "Don't wait for me," he said.

Wycza grinned under the hood. "Don't worry." He clambered out of the patrol car and ran around the truck cab.

They were all clustered there, Paulus and Kerwin and Wiss and Elkins. Wycza told them, "Get in. All in back, I got others to pick up."

Everybody moved but Paulus, who wasted time asking, "What's going on? What's happening?"

"Get in or I leave you."

Wycza got up in the cab, kicked the engine on, and pulled away from the curb. They'd taken the truck around the block when they'd first come in, so it would be facing the right way; he was grateful for that now.

He went four blocks and there was Grofield waiting for him, on a corner, without his hood. And not alone.

Wycza braked to a stop, and Grofield pulled open the door. Wycza said, "Get her the hell out of here!"

"She's coming along."

Wycza wouldn't agree to that for a second, but there wasn't time to argue. They were both in the cab, so he hit the accelerator again. "Parker'll kill you," he said.

"Let me worry about it."

The girl said, "Don't worry about me. You don't have to worry about me. What's going on?"

Grofield said, "We'll find out later, honey. Just be quiet now."

Wycza said, "Throw her out when we pick up Salsa. I'm telling you."

"She's coming along, so shut up, huh?"

"There's no room for Salsa."

"She'll sit on my lap."

Wycza ground his teeth in frustration. Of all the stupidities tonight, Edgars' had suddenly taken second place behind Grofield's. "I'm liable to kill you myself," he said, and stopped the truck again to pick up Salsa.

Salsa squeezed into the cab and reported, "No troopers yet."

They were all crammed in together, Grofield in the middle, the girl on his lap, the girl holding Wycza's walkie-talkie and Grofield's rifle. Salsa had a machine gun on the floor between his feet, and a walkie-talkie in his lap.

Wycza said, "Tell Parker it's still clear."

"Sure," said Salsa. He picked up the walkie-talkie.

"No sense telling him about the broad." Wycza turned his head and gave Grofield a cold eye, then looked front again. "He'll find out soon enough."

"Sure," said Salsa. The presence of the girl didn't seem to ruffle him a bit. He spoke into the walkie-talkie, saying, "Everything's clear so far. We're out of town, and no troopers have come in yet."

Parker's voice came out of both walkie-talkies in the cab: "I've got Littlefield and Phillips, I'm coming out now."

Wycza looked in the rear-view mirror. Behind him was the town. He saw flames shooting upward, deep within it, and way back on Raymond Avenue he saw a pair of headlights. "He'd better move," he muttered.

Ahead, on the right, was the trooper barracks, still lit up. As they passed it, they saw two men in uniform running from the front door toward one of the cars. Wycza said, "Salsa, keep an eye on them. See which way they go."

"Right."

Wycza's foot was heavy on the accelerator. The truck was

doing seventy now, and the speedometer was still creeping upward. He kept telling himself he should get down to the speed limit, but he couldn't lift his foot off the accelerator; it was as though his foot were nailed there.

He'd never taken a fall. He'd never spent even one night in jail. He kept thinking about that now, never a single night in jail. And he didn't want to go to jail, because he knew what would happen to him if he went to jail. He would die. A year, maybe two years, and he'd be dead.

There were things he needed, in order to stay alive. Food and shelter and water, of course, but other things, too, that for him were just as important. Exercise, for instance. He had to be able to run, to run for miles, and to do it every single day. He had to be able to go into a gym and work out whenever he wanted. He had to keep using his body, or it would dry up and die.

And women. He needed women almost as much as he needed exercise. Not in the goddam truck on the job, but other times, other places. And sunshine, plenty of sunshine. And certain kinds of food; steak, and milk, and green vegetables. And food supplements, vitamin pills and mineral pills and protein pills.

Not in jail. In jail, he wouldn't be able to exercise his body as much as was necessary. And there'd be no women. And little sunshine. And none of the foods or pills he needed. In jail, he would shrivel up like a leaf in September. He'd shrink and get pasty, his teeth would rot, his muscles would sag, his body would shrink in on itself and start to decay.

"They're going towards the town."

Wycza nodded. "Good. Tell Parker."

He wasn't going to jail. If it came down to it, if it ever came right down to it, he knew he wouldn't go to jail. There are two ways to die, fast and slow, and he'd prefer the fast way. He wouldn't go to jail because in order to put him in jail they'd have to lay hands on him, and before they'd be able to lay hands on him they'd have to kill him.

Salsa was talking to Parker on the walkie-talkie: "State police, coming in."

"Yeah, I see the red light. I'm going to park and let them go by."

Then the cab was silent. Everybody was listening, waiting for the walkie-talkies to speak again. Wycza glanced at the speedometer; five miles to go to the highway. Doing seventy-five now.

"They went by. They're headed for the fire. I'm coming out now."

Salsa said, "Fine. I can't see the barracks anymore, but I didn't see any other cars leave there."

"There's nothing coming this way. I just passed the town line."

Wycza realized he'd been hunching his shoulders over the wheel. He sat back now, and let them relax; they'd started to ache. He lifted his foot from the accelerator, and let the truck slow down to the speed limit.

"We made it anyway," he said.

The girl said, "You don't have to worry about me, you really don't."

"I'm not going to," Wycza told her. "Grofield is." Ahead was the highway turnoff.

10

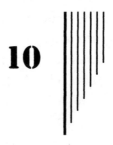

Four A.M.

Most of Copper Canyon was awake. The sidewalks were full of people, and other people were standing on their porches, and other people had got into their cars and were jamming up the streets around the fires.

There were three fires. Behind the plant fence, four buildings were aflame. On Caulkins Street, the firehouse was still burning, but was nearly out; the exterior walls, made of brick, were unharmed except for the chunk blown out by the hand grenade, but the interior of the building had been gutted. The square block bounded by Orange Street and Hector Avenue and Loomis Street and George Avenue was one mass of flame. The railroad station was in that block, and Ekonomee Gas, and a few other buildings, stores mostly, plus the garage and storage building of Elmore Trucking. Just at four o'clock, the fire leaped Loomis Street; two residences on the south side of the street caught fire as embers fell on their roofs.

The two state troopers had discovered the destruction of Copper Canyon's fire-fighting apparatus, had radioed to the barracks to have fire engines rushed in from Madison and Polk, and had entered police headquarters, baffled by the absence of all local police officials. Just at four A.M. they entered the Command Room and found the three bodies; all three were now dead.

In all the confusion, with the gigantic distraction of the triple fire, no one had yet noticed the broken windows and gaping doorways along Raymond Avenue.

Eight miles south, a brown tractor trailer was making the turn from 22A to the highway, eastbound. Two miles behind it a station wagon was speeding along at eighty miles an hour.

Three other cars were leaving the state trooper barracks two miles south of town, but all three of them were heading north, toward Copper Canyon.

Five A.M.

The three fires were one. The plant fire had moved south, and the Ekonomee fire had moved north, and they'd met at Caulkins Street, one block west of the firehouse. The suction of the fires was forcing winds into Copper Canyon from the south, fresh cold air rushing in to supply more oxygen for the flames, hot dry air blasting upward along the rear canyon wall. The direction of the wind confined the fire, for the most part, to the area north of Loomis Street, but nearly everything in an area three blocks wide and five blocks long was or had been aflame.

Fire engines from Madison and Polk had arrived half an hour ago. The firemen were primarily trying to contain the blaze, trying to keep it from stretching east and west of the area it had already consumed. The morning and evening shifts of the town police department had come out in uniform to help the state police maintain some sort of order, keeping the curious back out of harm's and the firemen's way.

Somebody had found Eddie Wheeler, and he'd been brought to one of the troopers, so now the law knew about the robberies, or at least some of them. The two women at the telephone company had been found and released, so now the law also knew that the robbers had taken a hostage with them. Eddie Wheeler had described the truck he'd seen, and state police cars were combing the highway and route 22A and other secondary routes in this part of the state, but they hadn't as yet found any brown truck. Two police helicopters were being readied at Bismarck, the state capital, and would be in the air shortly. Reporters and wire service stringers were driving pell-mell toward Copper Canyon from all over the state.

It would be late afternoon before the fire would be completely extinguished, and tomorrow morning before the rubble would have cooled enough to permit inspection. Bodies would be found in the ruins, and tentatively identified, but the body of Edgars would never be discovered; it had been too close to the hottest core of the fire. All the next day, merchants and accountants would be toting up figures, learning just exactly how much had been stolen in all. Police technicians would be dusting virtually the whole town for fingerprints, and would find none left by the robbers, but would be surprised that there were still on various surfaces in police headquarters fingerprints left by former Chief of Police Edgars, who'd left town nearly a year ago and was not likely to show his face here ever again.

The roadblocks would be left up for another day, to be on the safe side. The two helicopters would continue their search. The police expected to apprehend the responsible parties very soon.

Eddie Wheeler spent the rest of the week in his own bed, with a head cold. By the time he was well enough to get up and move around, Betty's parents were back in town.

Three days after the holocaust, two architects and a lawyer and a minister formed the Citizens for Copper Canyon, CCC. Their goal was to convince their fellow citizens to rebuild the gutted section of town according to this plan they'd whipped up. Copper Canyon Plaza. Official buildings here at this end, new railroad station at the other end, the fountain here, the gardens here, and so on. The architects would be happy to prepare plans for the new integrated area, and the lawyer would be happy to handle the legal work involved. The minister was selfless.

FOUR

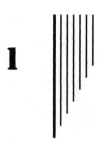

1

Parker watched Wycza drive the truck over to the edge and start it down the road to the bottom of the ravine. The loot was still in it; it would be light in an hour, so the best thing was to get the truck out of sight right away. Tomorrow night would be soon enough to make the split.

After the taillights had dropped down out of sight, he turned and went back toward the shed, thinking about the job. It had been beautiful. It could have been the cleanest and sweetest job he'd ever been in on. The closest thing to a foul-up was that night-owl kid that stumbled over Paulus working the bank. And that had turned out to be no problem; they'd handled it smooth and quiet and sweet. The whole thing was smooth and quiet and sweet, no killings, no messiness, no problems.

Except Edgars.

He'd known, God damn it, he'd known all along there was

something wrong with Edgars. Edgars and his personal reasons. Those personal reasons had to blow the whole job sky high, they *had* to.

It had still worked out. They'd had to leave a little of the take behind, dribs and drabs from a couple of store safes, nothing important. They'd had to do the job a hell of a lot faster than they'd planned. But still and all it had worked out. Chambers was dead, and Edgars was dead, and there was no telling how many locals were dead, but at least they'd managed to get themselves out from under with the loot.

The dead locals were what bothered him. He didn't give a damn one way or the other, not personally, couldn't care less if they'd lived or died, but it was never good to cut down a citizen in a robbery. There's trouble enough from the law if they're just after you for a payroll, but if they're after you for Murder One you're in big trouble.

He pushed open the door of the shed and looked in. They were all there, Paulus and Wiss and Elkins and Kerwin and Littlefield and Salsa and Grofield and Phillips.

And Grofield's girl, sitting with Grofield on one of the army cots.

Parker looked at her, and then looked at Grofield. Grofield had the look on his face that a man gets when he's done something too stupid to be possible and he knows it but still wants to justify it.

Parker motioned to him to come outside. Grofield murmured something at the girl and got to his feet. She made as though to come along, but he shook his head and murmured some more, and this time she nodded and sat down again on the army cot. Her hands were in her lap, her knees were together, and her face looked pinched and frightened. She looked like the heroine of a silent movie.

Parker stepped aside and let Grofield out, then followed him and shut the door. He led the way out toward the edge, walking forward through the dim starlight, the sheds bulking around him. He stopped near the edge and said, "You can bury her down there someplace."

"Forget it, Parker. You don't kill that girl."

"That's right, I don't. She's your responsibility."

"You don't have to worry about her, Parker." Grofield's voice had the shaky belligerence of a man who's pretty sure he's in the wrong but will be damned if he'll admit it.

"I'm not worrying about her, Grofield. *You* worry about her. In a day or two, she'll want to go home."

"No, she won't."

"When she tells you she's changed her mind, she wants to go home, but she'll never tell anybody where we are or what we look like or what our names are, that's when you take care of her."

"It won't happen. She won't say that."

"And you take her down there and bury her. Deep, Grofield. I don't want her found."

"What if it doesn't happen? What if she doesn't change her mind?"

"We'll be here three or four days. Then what?"

"New York. We'll get a place in the Village for the summer. In the fall we'll go south and do winter stock together. She's always wanted to be an actress."

"I always thought you were a pro."

"I am. I know what I'm doing."

Parker shook his head. "I didn't know I'd have to spell it all out for you. All right, listen."

"None of this is necessary, Parker, honest to Christ."

"Shut up and listen. You know how to keep the law off your tail. She doesn't. They'll pick her up for jaywalking in New York City, and before the cop gets the ticket wrote out she'll be so rattled she'll spill the whole works."

"No, she won't. She can learn."

"Shut up. There's just one thing. She'll louse up somehow, and get the law down on you. Number two, she'll change her mind. Maybe tomorrow, maybe six months from now. She thought it'd be exciting to run off with an honest-to-god bank robber, and how long you think she'll think it's exciting?"

"I can keep her interested, Parker. That girl's never been anywhere or done anything. I'll show her New York this summer, Miami this winter, a season of winter stock, maybe New England next summer, maybe after a while go out and try Hollywood. She won't get bored, believe me."

"No, she'll get homesick."

"Parker, listen. She told me about herself. Her folks are dead; she was living with her uncle. Just the two of them."

"That's another thing. She'll not only get homesick for the uncle, the uncle'll keep the law looking for her."

"No, he won't. She doesn't know it yet, but the uncle's dead. He was that fireman, that George."

Parker looked at him in the small light; too small to see his face. "You think that's good?"

"She's got no home to get sick for, no place to go back to."

"She'll want to be at the funeral, number one. Number two, you were part of the gang that killed him."

"That was Edgars, that wasn't us. I can tell her about that so she'll believe me. And so what about the funeral? I can keep her from even thinking about it."

"The other two women at the phone company know she went with you. The law know she's with us."

"She'll dye her hair. She wanted to anyway, but her uncle wouldn't let her. For Christ's sake, Parker, she's twenty-two years old, she's nobody's ward."

"I don't want her going back. I don't want her saying it was a guy named Parker and a guy named Grofield and a guy named this and that, and that's Grofield's picture there, and that's Phillips' picture there, and all that crap."

"She won't go back, Parker."

"I know that. I want to be sure *you* know it."

"Parker, I wouldn't have brought her along if I wasn't sure."

"Yeah. Go get her. Send her out here."

"Parker, I don't want you to lay a hand on her."

"That's not my job. That's your job. I want to talk to her."

Grofield shuffled his feet, and the silence lengthened between them until he finally said, "You going to tell her about her uncle?"

"Maybe."

"Then tell her about Edgars."

"Go get her, Grofield."

"Don't try to *push* her away, Parker."

"I won't. Go get her."

"All right."

Grofield took a few steps away, and then Parker called his name and said, "I want to see her alone first."

"I know. I figured that out already."

Parker looked up at the sky. Four-thirty in the morning, it was still fully night, but the stars seemed to be getting a bit fainter, the sky a bit less totally black. Except for the stars, there was no light anywhere; black cloth covered the windows of the shed they were living in.

There was a crunching sound from the left, opposite the shed. Parker listened to it, frowning, and then realized who it was. "Wycza," he said.

Wycza loomed up out of the darkness. "That's a long walk," he said.

"What do you think about Grofield's girl?"

"I think he's stupid."

"That's *him*. What about *her*?"

"I dunno. She doesn't yack a lot. He didn't have to twist her arm to bring her. I dunno about her."

"This could have been a sweet job."

"Tell me about that Edgars sometime."

"I wish I knew myself."

The girl was suddenly there, saying softly, "You wanted to talk to me?"

Parker turned and said, "Yeah. Wait there a second." He turned back to Wycza. "What happens if it rains out here?"

"You mean with the sheds?"

"Yeah."

"I guess they leak. But I don't think it rains here this time of year."

"Is that right?" Parker turned to the girl. "Does it rain here this time of year?"

"Not very often." Her voice was very low and soft, but not shy in particular, just self-contained. The frightenedness that had been in her face before was completely missing from her voice.

Parker didn't give a damn about rain or leaking sheds; he wanted to rattle her by talking at her instead of to her for a while, to see how she'd react. He said to Wycza, "What'll we do if it does rain? You got any ideas?"

"Not me."

He turned to the girl. "What about you? You got any ideas?"

"You robbed the banks, didn't you?"

He was alert now. "That's right," he said, and waited.

But what she said was, "They keep their money in those canvas sacks, don't they? You could cut them open and spread the sacks out on the roof on the parts where it leaks."

Wycza laughed, and said, "I'll be seeing you, Parker." He trudged away toward the shed.

Parker said, "They'll have helicopters out. We can't have bank sacks on the roof."

"Oh, I'm sorry. I didn't think of that."

"Did you ever hear of a guy named Edgars?"

"The man who used to be police chief?"

"That's the one."

"He was with you tonight, wasn't he?"

"What did he have against your town?"

"There was a big scandal. A grand jury asked him questions and tried to get evidence against him about something; I don't know exactly what. I don't think they ever tried him for anything, but he was dismissed anyway."

"That figures. He tried to blow up your whole damn city tonight."

"I saw the fires."

"Blew up part of the plant, and a gas station by the railroad depot, and the firehouse."

"The firehouse?"

"Killed the man I had in there guarding your uncle."

"Oh." She was silent, but he didn't have anything to say to her, he could outwait her. After a minute she said, "My uncle?"

"He got it, too. Everybody in the firehouse. The man I had in there was named Chambers. Hillbilly from Kentucky or somewhere like that. Has a brother named Ernie, in jail now. He's the one was supposed to drive the truck."

"What are you trying to do to me?"

He took a last drag on his cigarette, and flicked the butt out over the edge. "See if you'll crack."

"Why?"

"You know my name. You know my face. I don't want you going back and talking to the law."

"I see."

They waited again. Parker got out his cigarettes, lit one, then said, "You want one?"

"Yes, please."

He lit it for her. She looked up and studied his face in the matchlight, and when it was dark again she said, "The simplest thing would just be to throw me off the cliff here, wouldn't it?"

"It would."

"Why don't you? You're not afraid of Grofield."

"I don't kill as the easy way out of something. If I kill, it's because I don't have any choice."

"You mean self-defense."

"Wrong. I mean it's the only way to get what I want."

"Do you want me to promise I'll stay with Grofield forever? Maybe I will, maybe I won't. I know I won't go back to Copper Canyon, and there's no reason for me to go to the police."

"Why'd you come along with Grofield?"

"He's my chance. He's smart and exciting and fun, and he knows a lot of things. He can show me the whole world, and make it all fun. I had to scream and holler before he'd take me along, so don't blame him too much."

"Grofield'll be in jail within five years."

"Why do you say that?"

"Because he's impulsive. He's smart, but he doesn't always act smart. Also, he doesn't pay his income tax. Also, he spends too loose and works too often."

"So maybe I can help him, then."

Parker debated. He walked up and down along the cliff edge, thinking it out. The girl was a lot better than he'd expected. The only false note was that she'd run off in the first place, that she'd decided to come along with Grofield. She was too cool and sure of herself to be the run-off type. But maybe the running off was cool and methodical, too, maybe she was just running a calculated risk. Looked at that way, it made better sense.

And made her a better risk for him, too.

He said, "Go tell Grofield to show you where his car is. That's where you two will stay nights; we can't have you in the shed with the rest of us."

"All right. Thank you."

She went away, and Parker stayed outside awhile longer. Far to the east, a narrow band of faint lightness was beginning to mark the horizon. Parker walked back and forth, back and forth, unwinding, getting the tension out of his body and mind.

He'd never been involved with such a contradictory job in his life. A job where he deliberately put himself in a box with only one exit, but in this particular case it didn't matter. A job where everything went smooth and sweet and precise, right up to the end, and then all hell broke loose, with one madman going around trying to blow up the city and another madman bringing a girl along for the ride. But the first madman's explosions and fires helped to cover the getaway in spite of themselves, and the second madman's girl turned out to be a safe risk.

Thinking of the girl, he felt a quickening in his loins, the sudden return of desire that always followed a job. He walked back and forth, back and forth, smoking his cigarette, thinking of women, thinking about the next opportunity he'd have to get next to a woman.

Not Grofield's girl. Messing with another man's woman was always dangerous, and never more dangerous than while hiding out. Besides, she acted too cool and composed for his taste. He wanted something with more abandon to her.

He knew who, knew exactly who. Three or four days, and he'd go see her.

Somebody had to tell her Edgars wouldn't be showing up.

2

The helicopter passed over again with a great flapping sound, like a huge bird of prey, and everyone in the shed crouched instinctively lower and stared upward at the roof.

It was late afternoon, and stifling hot in the shed. They were all there, all eleven of them. Parker and Wycza and Phillips and Salsa and Elkins were sitting around the card table, a hand of seven-card stud half dealt in front of them, halted temporarily while they all listened to the helicopter. Grofield and his girl were sitting on an army cot in the corner, with Littlefield standing next to them; the three of them had been playing charades and Littlefield had stopped in the middle of the third word. Wiss and Paulus and Kerwin, the three safe men, had been shop-talking in a corner, but they too were now quiet.

Pop Phillips said, "It's enough to make a man think of re-forming."

"Tire tracks," said Parker. He looked over at Littlefield. "What about them?"

"Brushed away," Littlefield told him. "All brushed away."

Wycza said, "What about on the road going down, where I took the truck?"

"That's all hard-packed," Littlefield told him. "No tracks show."

Paulus said, "I don't like this place. Edgars set this place up, what do we know about it? We ought to get the hell out of here."

Parker shook his head. "And go where? None of us knows this territory. The roadblocks'll still be up."

"I just don't like this place. I want out of here tonight."

Parker shrugged and looked at his hole cards. Five and seven of spades. Six of spades and queen of hearts up, so far. Three cards to go.

Two days to go. This was always the worst part, afterward. The best jobs were the ones you could walk away from and keep on going. But the jobs where you had to hole up for a while, they were bad for the nerves. Particularly with a crowd this size. Eleven people stuck in a big empty shed with no interior walls, no proper furniture, no way to get away from each other. A lot of jobs that had run sweet all the way through suddenly went sour at this point, after the tough part was supposedly all over. One or two people decided not to wait it out anymore, took off, got themselves picked up and backtracked, and there was the law all of a sudden at the hide-out door.

Paulus said, "We make the split tonight, and then I go. Littlefield? You're supposed to ride with me, you want to come along?"

Littlefield seemed to consider it, and then said, "I don't think so, Paulus. I think I'll stay here and keep out of jail, if I can get a ride with somebody else."

Salsa said, "Chambers was supposed to ride with me. You can take his place."

"Thank you."

Paulus said, "Well, *I'm* going. Tonight, right after the split."

Parker, looking at his cards, said, "We don't split tonight. We make the split day after tomorrow."

Paulus said, "I'm taking *my* share tonight."

Wycza said, "Shut your face, Paulus, you ain't going nowhere."

"I don't *like* this place, I tell you!"

Grofield said, "Shut up a second. Listen. Is he coming back?"

The sound of the helicopter had faded to a murmur, but that murmur had remained unchanged as the copter circled the general area over the mining cut. Now the murmur was getting louder again.

Phillips said, "What does he think he *sees* out there?"

Nobody answered him. The murmur increased and then faded again, without having come close. It faded almost out of hearing, and then came back a little, and then faded again.

Salsa said, "He'd doing a grid-check, that's all. A methodical search pattern. These sheds were a landmark for him, a hub, but now he's got some other hub."

"I hope you're right," said Phillips.

They listened some more. The helicopter was a distant hum, and then silence. Very briefly, a humming again, like a far-off bee, and then silence. Still silence. Silence.

Parker said, "Deal. He's gone."

Elkins picked up the cards and dealt another round. Parker got the jack of spades. He called Phillips' bet without raising, and got the four of spades on the sixth card. He bumped small, fed Phillips' large return raise, bet more heavily after the last card, and took the pot.

Paulus said, "I'm going tonight, and I'm going with my piece of the score."

Parker and Wycza looked at each other. It was Wycza who said it: "You're staying here, Paulus, and we're making the split the day after tomorrow. Now shut your trap about it."

Paulus shut his trap, but he looked mutinous.

Grofield guessed Littlefield's charade: "'All the world's a stage, and all the men and women merely players.'"

Phillips took the next pot. Raking it in, he said, "'All things come to him who waits.'"

"That's the tough part," Parker told him.

3

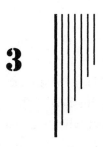

Parker came awake all at once to find Wycza's hand on his shoulder. Wycza whispered, "Paulus."

Parker nodded and got to his feet. The shed was full of the hushes of sleeping breath. Cots were placed every which way around the room, and men were sleeping on all of them.

Wycza whispered, "Salsa, too?"

Parker nodded.

They moved forward, and Wycza touched Salsa's shoulder. Salsa too came straight awake and sat up. Wycza whispered Paulus' name, and then the three of them went outside and shut the shed door behind them.

It was cool at night here, and tonight there was a dampness in the air that hadn't been present before. The stars were obscured, the sky heavy and black.

Parker whispered, "Where?"

"I heard him when he started the car. He took it down below."

"Gone to get his share."

"Yeah."

Salsa said, "He may start up before we can get down. He'll be tough to get hold of, in his car."

Parker said, "Is there any other way out of there?"

Wycza shook his head. "Just this one road. Chambers and I looked that over when we first came out."

"We can block it at the top with one car."

"Okay, good."

They went to the shed where they'd stashed the wagon, and pulled the corrugated sections of wall away, moving as silently as they could. The darkness was almost complete. Parker backed the wagon out, turning the parking lights on and with that small illumination drove over to the dropoff and the beginning of the road down to the bottom. He left the wagon parked across the road at the very top, pointing out into space. He switched the lights off and climbed out, and rejoined Wycza and Salsa, a little way off, standing at the edge over the road. They stood there and waited.

"Here he comes," said Salsa.

Wycza said, "The damn fool's using his parking lights."

Salsa said, "I wouldn't try to come up that without light."

They waited. The car crept slowly upward and was almost to the wagon before it stopped. The parking lights went out immediately. Paulus didn't make a sound.

Whispering, Wycza asked, "What do we do with him?"

"I don't want to have to bury him," said Parker.

"We tie him and leave him on one of the cots," said Salsa. "Grofield's girl can feed him."

"I don't work with him again," said Wycza. "That much I know."

Paulus' voice came up to them suddenly, with startling loudness, "Get that car out of the way!"

"Forget it, Paulus."

"I'll ram it!"

Salsa squatted down on his heels and called softly down to Paulus: "Don't make things so difficult for yourself. Come back to the shed and we'll tie you up a few days."

"There'll be law here by tomorrow! Edgars set us up to be collared, don't you damn fools *see* that?"

Salsa said, "You're all excited, Paulus. Don't they know we have rifles, machine guns? Don't they know how many of us there are? If they thought we were in here, would that helicopter pilot come back two-three times all by himself and down so low?"

"Why'd he come back, then?"

"Paulus, you don't know anything about search patterns, do you?"

"This place is naked, we stick out like boils. I want to be away from here, a thousand miles away from here."

Parker was tired, and a little chilly. He wanted to be back asleep. He said, "Quit screwing around, Paulus, you aren't going anywhere."

"God damn you, Parker!"

The headlights of Paulus' car came on all at once, on high beam, flooding the station wagon with light, light reflecting away on all sides to show Parker and Wycza standing big and heavy by the edge, Salsa hunkered down like a bandit beside them, the three looking down over the edge at the car just below them. Paulus' car was so close, they could have stepped down onto the roof.

The car began to back, Paulus gunning the engine. Salsa called something to him, but the roaring of the engine drowned it out. The car backed downward, and then they could see Paulus at the steering wheel, facing backward, twisted around and straining to see. There was only darkness behind the car, tinged with red by the taillights.

Paulus was excited, so maybe he forgot to reverse the turning direction on the steering wheel when going backward. Or maybe he just couldn't see well enough back there. His left rear wheel went off the edge.

Salsa hollered, "Jump!"

Parker dropped down to the road surface, landing on his hands and feet, going down to his knees and getting up again.

But Paulus was on the wrong side of the car to jump. And the engine was still roaring, so his foot was still heavily on the accelerator. The car seemed to tremble a minute, while Parker ran down toward its headlights, and then it swung sharp left, the front of the car with its blinding headlights snapping out into space to stare out over the ravine, and then it dropped.

Parker was running back up the other way long before they heard the crashing sound down below. He ran up to the wagon, and Wycza and Salsa were there. He said, "Wycza, get Phillips. Have him show you the shovels. Get Elkins and come down, bring a car. Salsa, let's go."

They got into the wagon, and Parker backed it away from the edge, then turned the wheel hard and they started down. Parker had the parking lights on again and went as far as he could.

Salsa, sitting on the outside near the cliff, said, "It's burning."

"We got to put it out."

"That Paulus was a real chancy type."

"He always tensed up, always."

"I guess none of us works with him again, huh?" Salsa grinned. "You sure get the interesting jobs, Parker."

"Crap."

At the bottom they made the U-turn. Paulus' wreck was ahead of them, outlined by flames; it looked like a mound of black spare parts.

It wasn't much of a fire; by the time Parker and Salsa got there the only things left burning were the upholstery and the roof padding and the body hanging halfway out the front seat.

"He's taking it with him," said Salsa. "His split, you know?"

Parker was down on one knee, feeling the ground, trying to find loose sand. "We got to get that fire *out*."

"Wait, Parker. Here they come with the shovels."

The other car was coming. Wycza and Elkins climbed out and passed out shovels. The four of them started digging, throwing dirt generally on the wreck and especially on the parts that were still burning. When the fire was put out, they brought the two cars closer in and switched on their parking lights to see by. Then they kept shoveling.

They moved around, not taking too much dirt from any one place, spreading it out so the ground wouldn't look more than usually uneven. When they were done, the mound of earth over the wreck was nearly waist high, but it would look all right from the air.

"One thing," said Elkins, "now it's a nine-way split."

"He took his with him," said Salsa. He seemed pleased by the remark.

4

The stink of sulphur was everywhere. In the dimness of twilight, the red waters of the stream looked a dark maroon, and velvety. Parker threw a machine gun into the stream and watched the bubbles rise, then turned back to the station wagon.

Grofield was coming over with the two rifles, wrinkling his nose. " 'I counted two-and-seventy stenches, all well defined, and several stinks.' "

Parker shrugged. He wasn't talking; when he opened is mouth he smelled the stink more.

The rear of the wagon was still full of revolvers. Parker picked up four of them by the trigger guards and carried them over to the stream and threw them in. Nobody'd stumble over them here, not too readily.

The guns could have been kept, but it would have been a false economy, and maybe dangerous. Until the next job, none of them would be needing a gun, and certainly not a rifle or chopper. In the meantime, they were difficult to transport, difficult to hide, and a cheap little rap if the law happened to stumble across them. So guns were just part of the overhead, bought before each job and got rid of afterward. Sometimes, if the job was done somewhere close to someone like Scofe, the blind man, or Amos Klee, the guns were sold back again at half price, but only if that was the easiest way to get rid of them.

After they'd all been dumped into the sulphurous stream, Parker and Grofield drove the station wagon over to the truck. Wycza and Salsa and Elkins were there, dragging the bags and trays of the score down to the end of the truck by the open doors. Parker swung the wagon around and backed it up to the rear of the truck, and then he and Grofield got out and started transferring the stuff from truck to wagon. There was another car there, too; when they finished filling the wagon they loaded the rest into the trunk of the other car.

This was the third day. Tonight, if everything was clear, they'd leave this place. The sky was overcast and heavy, had been all day, building up from a lighter cloudiness yesterday. It hadn't rained yet; with luck, it wouldn't for a day or two.

Parker and Grofield and Wycza rode up in the station wagon, and the other two in the car. When they passed the mound of dirt covering Paulus' wreck, Grofield said, "If it rains, the dirt'll get washed away."

"You got any ideas?"

"No. I was just saying."

Parker grunted. What was the sense of talking about a problem if you didn't have a way to solve it?

They drove up to the top and unloaded the two cars, carrying everything into the shed. Phillips and Littlefield and Wiss and Kerwin came out to help, making it like a bucket brigade, passing the sacks and bags and trays from hand to hand, piling it all up in a corner of the shed. Grofield's girl sat on an army cot and watched it mount up. In the last few days, sleeping in Grofield's car, with no fresh clothes to change to, she'd got a little bedraggled-looking, but it didn't really hurt her appearance. She'd got, if anything, sexier-looking now. Parker had seen Salsa and a couple of the others looking at her. If they couldn't all leave here tonight, there might be trouble yet.

When the cars were unloaded, Parker and Wycza put them back in their sheds and put the sides up, then went back to the living shed, where the others had started the count.

They'd taken nothing but money. They'd left the jewelry store stock alone because the only way to make a profit on jewelry was to sell it back to the insurance company covering the store's loss, and in an operation like this, with so much other stuff taken, it would be too risky to try to get in touch with the insurance companies. As for the money, they'd taken only bills, leaving all sacks of change. Change was too heavy to carry, too bulky for the value, and too awkward to spend.

It took a long time to make the count; and outside, evening became a night. The black curtains were put up in front of the windows and the electric lanterns were lit, and they went on counting. Their final total was $294,660.

Next, Grofield made his accounting of the $4,000 front money. He had a list of who had got how much and for what, and he had $730 left. He added $7,270 to it from the score to make the $8,000 that was to be paid to the doctor in New York. The $8,000 was put in an unmarked canvas sack and given to Grofield to deliver.

That left $287,390. Phillips got out pencil and paper and did the long division, and it came out $31,932.22. "Plus a fraction," Phillips told them. "Two two two, it keeps going on."

They worked it out. If each man took $31,900 there'd be $290 left over. Salsa said, "Give it to Grofield for a wedding present." He bowed and smiled at Grofield's girl.

That was the way they did it. Salsa presented the girl with the $290, making a little ceremony out of it. Parker watched Grofield watching Salsa, but Salsa didn't push it, and the tense minute passed.

When the split was finished, Phillips got ready to leave. His cut was still sitting on the card table, not yet claimed. He put on an old black-and-red-check hunting jacket and a gray cap, and then he looked exactly like a dairy farmer getting ready to go out and milk the cows. He stuck a pipe in his mouth to complete the picture and went out to get the station wagon, which was dirty enough by now to add to the general picture. He drove off in the wagon, and the rest settled down to wait. Phillips was the best man to try this because he looked the least like a desperado. He was to drive around the general area—but not too close to Copper Canyon—and see if things had quieted down yet or not. When he came back, he'd tell them if it was safe to leave here. If he didn't come back, that would be an answer, too.

While he was gone, Parker and Wycza took shovels over to one of the sheds with a dirt floor and dug a deep hole and buried the money sacks and trays in it. The others were gathering up the gear in the living shed, getting ready to move it out if Phillips said everything was okay.

He was gone three hours. It was a little after eleven when he came back, his headlights gleaming ahead of him. He left the wagon in front, came into the shed, and said, "As clear as water. No roadblocks or anything. I heard on the radio where they think we escaped into Canada already."

"That's the one direction none of us goes," said Parker. "They'll still be watching the border."

Phillips got his little cardboard suitcase and shoveled his share of the score into it. They all had suitcases or bags of one kind or another for their part of the loot.

They all worked together, moving all the equipment out of the shed and loading it into the station wagon. Army cots, the card table and folding chairs, cartons of rubbish, unused food, everything went into the station wagon, filling it from front to back with just enough room for Phillips to get behind the wheel. He drove it down to put it with the truck, and Wycza took his own car and followed, to drive Phillips back up.

They got their cars out of the sheds and, using as little

light as possible, arranged the sheds to look the same as when they'd come here. Sooner or later the truck and station wagon would be found, but they were at the bottom where, because of the fumes, people were less likely to go. Hunters or kids or whatnot might come around these sheds up at the top anytime. It might be months before the truck and wagon were found, and even then there was nothing in either to connect them directly with the score. Unless the law had one or the other identified, maybe when they'd driven out.

They left at fifteen-minute intervals, Wycza and Phillips first. Kerwin and Grofield and Grofield's girl left in the second car, and Wiss and Elkins in the third, and Salsa and Littlefield in the fourth.

Parker was last. He took one more look around, then loaded his luggage into the trunk of the Mercury. It was one o'clock Monday morning. Parker drove out to the highway and turned east.

5

The blonde looked past him and said, "Where's Edgars?"

"He isn't coming." Parker pushed on by her and dropped his suitcase on the floor. The room was stuffy, smelling of woman and alcohol. The windows were closed, the venetian blinds shut, the drapes pulled. The sun was shining outside, but she had the lights on in here.

She shut the door after him and said, "What happened to him?" She seemed sober, or close enough to it. She was wearing a blue robe, and she was barefoot; red nail polish was half chipped off her toenails.

Parker said, "He died. Open a window."

"I like the windows shut. How come he died?"

"Because he was a damn fool." Parker went over to a window, yanked the drapes aside, pulled the blinds up, and opened the window all the way. A cool breath of fresh air came in.

"You move right in, don't you?"

"You been out of this room at all?"

"What do you care?"

Parker crossed the room and opened the other window. Now a breeze came through, clearing out the underground aura.

She said, "You killed him, huh?"

"No. He killed himself."

"That big hooraw at Copper Canyon, that was you people, wasn't it?"

"What big hooraw?"

She shrugged and went over to the dresser, where the bottle and glass were. She poured and said, "What do I care if he's alive or dead?"

"He was sick in the head. He tried to blow up the whole town, and one of his grenades knocked a wall over on him."

"What was the matter with him?"

"He had a peeve against the town. We had a nice quiet operation going, and all of a sudden he blew up. Killed one of the boys, and a lot of locals, started fires all over the place, and got himself killed by a wall."

She shook her head, a sour grin on her face. "I pick 'em, don't I? Tell me, Parker, what's wrong with you?"

"There's nothing wrong with me."

"There's got to be something, Parker, or I wouldn't pick you."

"You didn't pick me. Get another glass."

"Oh, don't act so goddam tough. Where are you going from here?"

"Drive to Chicago, take a plane to Miami. You like Miami?"

"How the hell do I know? This is the farthest I've ever been from New York in my life."

Parker looked at her, and thought of Grofield's girl. Where do you find one like that? Forget it, there'd be something wrong with her, too. He stretched and said, "Get the glass, I'm thirsty."

"Will you treat me nice? Will you for Christ's sake treat me nice?"

He looked at her. "What happens if I treat you nice?"

"How do I know? Nobody ever did. Maybe I turn into a butterfly."

"Let's find out. Come here."

She put the glass down on the dresser and came over. There was a pensive expression on her face, and she seemed oddly shy. It was out of character.

He reached for her, and she said, "The windows are all open."

"Will you forget the goddam windows?"

"All right. Anything you say."

His hands removed her robe. "Butterfly. Sure."

PARKER NOVELS BY RICHARD STARK

The Hunter {Payback}
The Man with the Getaway Face
The Outfit
The Mourner
The Score
The Jugger
The Seventh
The Handle
The Rare Coin Score
The Green Eagle Score
The Black Ice Score
Deadly Edge
The Blackbird
Slayground
Lemons Never Lie
Plunder Squad
Butcher's Moon
Comeback
Backflash
Flashfire
Firebreak
Ask the Parrot
Dirty Money